COPY 1

D0465363

Quincy Rumpel, P.I.

Quincy Rumpel, P.I.

Betty Waterton

A Groundwood Book
Douglas & McIntyre
TORONTO/VANCOUVER

Groundwood Books/ Douglas & McIntyre Ltd.
26 Lennox Street, 3rd Floor
Toronto, Ontario M6G 1J4

Canadian Cataloguing in Publication Data

Waterton, Betty
    Quincy Rumpel, P.I.

ISBN 0-88899-081-2

I. Title.

PS8595.A73Q56 1988   jC813'.54   C88-094092-1
PZ7.W37Qui 1988

Design by Michael Solomon
Cover art by Eric Beddows
Printed and bound in Canada

1 2 3 4 5 6 7 8 9 6 5 4 3 2 1 0 9 8

To Sara and Chris

With special thanks
to Shelley Tanaka

1

"No, seriously! I don't think it's too soon to start thinking about our future. We'll soon be teen-agers, you know."

Quincy had stopped off at Gwen's house on her way home from school. Now she lay sprawled on top of her cousin's bed, feet crossed over the white head-board. Clasping her wrists with either hand, she squeezed rhythmically, causing her baggy grey sweatshirt to quiver slightly.

"I don't think that's helping much, you know," said Gwen, glancing briefly at Quincy. "Those chest ex-pansion exercises, I mean." Swooping her blonde hair over to one side, she studied the effect critically in the mirror above her bureau. "Do you like my hair on one side like this?"

Quincy grunted. Recrossing her long legs in their rumpled grey sweatpants, she took off her rosy-tinted glasses and peered intently at her left hand.

"Now what are you doing? Have you got a sliver or something?"

"I'm trying to read my destiny. My curvy line is really long, but it has a lot of little doodads on it. I wonder what that means?"

"Maybe you don't want to know. Please get your feet off my Michael J. Fox poster!"

Quincy's grubby sneakers shifted slightly. "Maybe it means I'll have a long life with lots of exciting adventures along the way! Maybe I'll be a journalist and travel all over. On the other hand, I might join the Mounties, probably the horse section . . ."

"Personally, I expect to do something humanitarian. Like Mother Theresa. I'll probably start by being a nurse. I look rather good in white." Reaching for her comb, Gwen parted her hair in the middle and pulled it back severely. As several curly little blonde tendrils escaped from her fingers, she sighed. "You're so lucky, Quince, not to have hair like this!"

"I could stand it," muttered Quincy, whose own straight red locks lay sparsely on the pink quilt.

"On the other hand," continued Gwen, tousling her hair over one eye, "it wouldn't be half bad to be a model and wear fabulous clothes. By the way, do you want to come to the Mall on Saturday? The February sales are still on."

"Got no money."

"We could window-shop."

"I'm sure not going to waste a whole Saturday window-shopping!" Swinging her legs off the bed, Quincy sat up. "What we need is a long weekend. Do you realize we don't have a national holiday in February?

You'd think they could at least declare Valentine's Day one! Of course, maybe the little kids wouldn't have quite so much fun. They probably wouldn't have valentine boxes at school anymore. But they'd get over it.''

"I love valentine boxes," said Gwen dreamily. "This year I got a fancy bought valentine with two hearts and a cupid on it, and a little plastic arrow. It cost two dollars — I know, because the price was on the back.''

"I got one of those, too, from Grandma Rumpel.''

"Mine wasn't from Grandma Rumpel. It was from Freddie Twikenham.''

Quincy's mouth fell open. "From Freddie? I don't believe it! How do you know? Did he sign it?''

"Practically.'' Giving her hair a final pat, Gwen shrugged off her powder-blue sweater and hung it in her closet.

"I'd sure like to see it," said Quincy. "Have you still got it?''

"It's probably around somewhere.'' Going directly to her pink-and-white desk, Gwen opened a drawer. She reached under a box of new pencils and pulled out a large envelope. Inside was a lace-trimmed valentine with two red hearts joined together by a gold-coloured plastic arrow. In a billowy cloud over the arrow floated a plump pink cupid.

Quincy grabbed the valentine and flipped it over to see the back. *"From Y.S.A.F. dot, dot, dot, et cetera; T. dot, dot, dot, et cetera.* That could stand for anything!''

"I decoded it. It stands for Freddie Twikenham, of course. Freddie likes using codes and things."

"Huh. But it could also stand for 'your sweet and friendly teacher'!"

"That's the stupidest thing you've ever said, Quincy Rumpel! I think you're jealous." Snatching the valentine out of Quincy's hand, Gwen put it back in the drawer under the box of pencils.

"Jealous? Moi? Over Fat Freddie? Don't make me laugh!" Grabbing her backpack, Quincy flounced out of the room, her flushed face nearly as red as her hair. She marched down the hall and out the front door, being careful, however, not to slam it. She knew Aunt Ida was in the kitchen.

She was just going through the white picket gate when Gwen stuck her head out the window and yelled after her, "And besides, nobody calls him that anymore!"

Quincy pretended not to hear. "You forgot your glasses!" Gwen shouted to her again. After that the window banged shut.

"Jeepers creepers," muttered Quincy. She turned around and stomped back to the house. Letting herself in, she retrieved her glasses from Gwen's bed and put them on. Her cousin was nowhere in sight.

From the kitchen came the rattle of pans and the sound of voices. "Is that you, Quincy?" called Aunt Ida. "Come on in and have a cookie!" Quincy paused, her hand on the doorknob. She hadn't the slightest desire to see Gwen at that moment, but there was an

10

enticing spicy smell wafting through the air. Lifting her nose, Quincy sniffed noisily. Then she sighed and headed for the kitchen.

Aunt Ida was packing some cookies into a small chocolate box, while Gwen sat at the table, munching. She didn't look up.

"Help yourself, dear," said Aunt Ida, pointing to some cookies cooling on a rack. Ignoring Gwen, Quincy did.

"These are dynamite ginger snaps, Aunt Ida."

Aunt Ida was small and cheerful, like her kitchen. Her apron matched the kitchen curtains, as did the potholders and the tea towel. They all had borders of little coffee pots and pepper grinders.

"Thank you, dear. I wanted some to take to Mrs. Beanblossom at the nursing home tomorrow. That dear old soul is always so grateful. She doesn't have much, you know."

"Is she the Mrs. Beanblossom from the old empty house down the street from us?" wondered Quincy. "That's a really spooky place!"

"Yes. The one on the waterfront. They say it used to be beautiful when the old captain was alive. They had their very own gardener and everything, and the grounds were a real showpiece. But now it's all overgrown, and the cliff is starting to crumble away into the sea."

"Erode," said Gwen, brushing some crumbs off her black stretch pants. "Why doesn't she sell it?"

"It doesn't really belong to her," replied her mother. "It has something to do with an estate in England.

Anyway, it's all tied up in red tape. Her furniture was sold, though, because she needed the money. They had some interesting pieces from the Orient, I understand. And for a while Mrs. Beanblossom kept insisting there was some kind of treasure at the house, but nothing was ever found.''

Quincy's hand, in the process of reaching for another ginger snap, wavered in mid air. ''I'll bet it was a buried treasure!'' she cried. Behind her pink glasses, her blue eyes gleamed. ''Did she say if it was a *buried* treasure?''

''I don't think she ever said. And now of course the old dear seems to have forgotten all about it.''

''Probably Alzheimer's,'' said Gwen.

''Mom forgets things all the time, and she doesn't have Alzheimer's,'' snapped Quincy. Then, turning to her aunt, she asked, ''What happened to Captain Beanblossom?''

''I think he disappeared mysteriously at sea somehow. It was before we moved to Tulip Street. I only met Mrs. Beanblossom lately when our Ladies Whistling Choir visited the nursing home to do a concert . . . . Why don't you ask Mrs. Murphy next door to you? She's lived in the neighbourhood a long time.'' Aunt Ida finished packing the ginger snaps. Leaving a few for the girls, she put the rest away in a large egg-shaped cookie jar, then started out of the kitchen.

''That's a good idea. I'll do it tonight. I'd love to find a treasure for that old lady! I wonder what could have happened to Captain Beanblossom? Maybe there was a mutiny on his ship, and he was cast adrift, like Henry Hudson. Or maybe they were hijacked by—"

"You can't just go snooping around other people's property," protested Gwen, taking a carton of milk from the fridge.

"You can if it's for somebody's good."

"You'll get into trouble." Gwen poured herself a glass of milk. "Do you want some?"

Quincy hesitated, but only briefly. "Don't mind if I do. I'm croaking after all those cookies." She helped herself to a glass from the cupboard. "I won't get into trouble. Maybe I'll get a search warrant or something."

"A search warrant? How could you get one of those?"

"Well, maybe not a search warrant. But I'll figure out something. All my life I've been waiting for a chance like this!" Quincy downed her milk and swished the glass quickly under the tap. "Thanks. Well, I'm on my way to talk to Mrs. Murphy and get things rolling. See you around!"

On her way to the front door, she noticed that Gwen was following her. "Do you want some help? Looking for the treasure, I mean?" Gwen asked.

Quincy considered. While it would be gratifying to find the treasure on her own, the old Beanblossom place was pretty spooky. It wouldn't hurt to have company. "Sure, I guess so," she said. "But just us two. Nobody else, understood?"

"Understood!"

"Okay, I'll get back to you on it. First I have to get the details."

13

Clutching her backpack in one hand, Quincy leaped energetically over the fence. Then she galloped down Tulip Street towards home, her mind a-whirl with sailing ships, crumbling cliffs and chests of buried treasure.

2

At the bottom end of Tulip Street, Quincy careened in behind a scraggly holly hedge to where the Rumpel house rose grandly, albeit with a slight list, a full two-and-a-half storeys. Every time Quincy saw the house, she felt a pang of pride. The brown shingles badly needed painting, and the front verandah sagged at one end, but none of this mattered to the Rumpels. They had moved in joyfully a year earlier after arriving from Ontario, enchanted by the house's nearness to the beach, and its handsome cherry tree. It also boasted, over the front door, a stained-glass window depicting a somewhat startled-looking seagull. The entrance was further enhanced by the Rumpels' genuine Swiss cowbell, which they had brought with them and which now hung by the door.

Taking the front steps two at a time, Quincy rattled the handle impatiently. It was locked, but loud music was coming from inside, so she rang the cowbell vigorously and pounded on the door. Eventually it opened a crack. A small pale face peered out cautiously.

"Morris!" screeched Quincy. "Let me in!"

Suddenly a huge white hairy dog covered with big black spots came hurtling out and flung himself into Quincy's arms.

"Snowflake! Baby! I've missed you, too!" cried Quincy, hugging him. Then she pushed her way into the house.

"So why are you barricaded in like this?" she demanded, as her little brother bolted the door behind her.

At seven, Morris was the youngest of the Rumpels. His father claimed that though he had the gentle brown eyes of a poet, he had the soul of a financier.

Turning down the radio, Morris whispered, "I'm cleaning my money."

The dining-room curtains were pulled. On the table, under the single dangling light bulb (which Mr. Rumpel intended to replace some day with a fancier fixture), was a pile of gold-coloured coins.

"Wow. Where did you get those?" gasped Quincy.

"Ha! Fooled you, didn't I?" grinned Morris, spraying her generously through the gap in his front teeth. Picking up a wooden spoon, he commenced stirring something in a bowl. Quincy bent down to see. In the bottom of the bowl was a little heap of dark-brown pennies.

"What are you using to clean them?" she asked.

"I'm not telling. It's a secret."

"So keep it, then. See if I care." Quincy headed for the kitchen.

"My other tooth came out today in school!" Morris sprayed after her.

"Big deal!"

Leah, the middle Rumpel child, was nine. Quincy found her seated comfortably at the kitchen table, engrossed in a horse magazine from the library.

"I thought you were supposed to be making supper," she said. "Mom will be home soon, and it's not even started."

"Where have you been? You're supposed to help, too."

"F.Y.I., I've been discussing something vastly more important at Gwen's." Quincy heaved her backpack onto the kitchen floor and tossed her ski jacket on top of it.

"What's F.Y.I.?" came Morris's shrill voice from the dining room.

"For your information, it means, For Your Information," shouted Leah.

"Who's been using the vinegar and baking soda?" asked Quincy, dumping a bag of potatoes into the sink.

"Nobody!" screeched Morris, appearing suddenly and snatching his secret ingredients off the counter.

Handing her sister the potato scraper, Quincy said, "Start peeling!" Then, taking a pair of yellow swim goggles from a drawer, she put them on and proceeded to chop onions for the hamburger, talking non-stop all the while. Before long, Leah had been completely briefed on the Beanblossom case (as Quincy was already thinking of it).

"And so," she concluded, "we're going to have a totally all-woman investigation. I guess you can be in it, too," she added graciously.

"Thanks," said Leah, tears streaming down her cheeks from Quincy's onions. "But what if Mom won't let us go looking around for buried treasure?" With Mr. Rumpel out of town selling his mini-trampolines, both girls knew that their mother would be the final and undisputed authority.

"Hey, don't worry about a thing," Quincy assured her sister. "*I* can handle Mom."

* * *

"Absolutely not!" said Mrs. Rumpel when she came home.

"There are laws about digging up other people's property — or there should be, if there aren't."

"But, Mom, we don't even know it's a *buried* treasure! It might just be sitting right there in the open. We only want to go and look around, for poor old Mrs. Beanblossom's sake!"

"Yeah, Mom," added Morris, sidling into the kitchen. "We'd even give her part of the treasure, wouldn't we, Quincy?"

"You've sure got big ears," sighed Quincy. "Yes, of course we'd give Mrs. Beanblossom the treasure. Or most of it, anyway."

"*All* of it," corrected Mrs. Rumpel, turning the hamburgers over.

"That means we can go and look?" Quincy beamed.

"If you're so determined to do this, why don't you go and talk to Mrs. Beanblossom herself about it?"

"Aunt Ida says she's too frail and her memory's not very good. Anyway, I've never been to a nursing home. All those old people would make me nervous."

"Quincy Rumpel, I'm ashamed of you!" said her mother. "I think I'll go and visit Mrs. Beanblossom myself — I didn't realize one of our neighbours might be lonely."

"Mrs. Murphy has lived here a long time and knows everybody. I'm going to start by talking to her," said Quincy, jumping up from the table.

"But not now." Mrs. Rumpel's voice was firm. "Nobody's going anywhere tonight. Leah has five blouses in the ironing pile and, Quincy, you were supposed to clean the bathroom last weekend and it's not done yet. I'd like it done tonight."

"Oh, gross!" moaned Quincy.

"But I don't need those blouses till next week," protested Leah. "I can borrow Quincy's frog sweater tomorrow."

"Oh, no, you can't. I'm wearing it myself."

"I'm too young to do any work," said Morris. "I'll go and talk to Mrs. Murphy."

"*You* get in there and pick up those pennies! And then you and I will do the dishes together. Also, your room needs tidying. I couldn't even find your bed this morning."

"But, Ma, my other tooth came out today. Maybe it's even still bleeding! I can't work that hard!"

"You heard me, Morris."

After that, nobody hung around the supper table. Morris scuttled into the dining room to attend to his money, and the two girls disappeared upstairs out of their mother's way.

"What do you think is the matter with Mom?" asked Leah, when they reached the safety of their bedroom. "Do you suppose working part-time is making her bossy?"

"Who knows," shrugged Quincy. "Maybe it's just because Dad's away and we're too much for her. She is getting kind of old to have three kids. We'll just have to humour her till Dad gets back."

The girls' bedroom at the back of the Rumpel house had two high, old-fashioned windows facing into the cherry tree, and a tiny balcony overlooking the back lane. Some former occupant had hung flowered wallpaper, and the giant blue and yellow pansies, though somewhat faded, still looked cheerful.

A recent addition of a bamboo curtain down the centre of the room divided it roughly in half. "It will be just like having separate bedrooms!" the girls had enthused, during the period when they were persuading their father to install it. Once installed, however, the curtain remained, for the most part, hoisted.

Precisely in the middle and against one wall stood a shared dresser. On one side of the room was a neatly made bed, a small desk and a bookcase tidily filled with dolls, stuffed animals, horse ornaments, books and a large jar of marbles. Over the bed was a poster of a mare and foal peacefully grazing. On the bed was a lace-trimmed cushion with *Leah* embroidered in pink.

On the other side of the room, under a poster of galloping horses, was a bed awash in a welter of blankets, clothes and frazzled stuffed animals. A bookcase was jammed with books, shoes, gym equipment and a plastic bag filled with Snowflake's wool. Dangling from the wall among old birthday cards and school pictures were three puppy collars of varying sizes (Snowflake had grown rapidly), a shrunken balloon with the tiny words *Expo '86*, a faded corsage from Quincy's first (and so far, only) dance, and a Save-the-Whales T-shirt. This last item was anchored by the shoulder seams so as to best display the treasured but unwashable autograph of an almost-famous track star. A Mickey Mouse alarm clock reposed on the night table beside a large bottle of Sparklewhite Dog Shampoo, while tacked to the ceiling overhead was a chart depicting possible locations of sunken pirate ships.

''We'd better have a meeting right now about this case,'' said Quincy, plopping herself down on Leah's bed. ''I think I'll run this treasure search like a real investigation. We should have a name, like a detective agency. What do you think of 'Rumpel Gumshoes'?''

''It sounds dopey.''

''Well, maybe I can think of something else.'' Pushing her glasses up on her head, Quincy proceeded to concentrate. Leah sat watching her.

Suddenly Mrs. Rumpel's voice broke the silence. "Quincy, have you finished the bathroom yet? I'm coming up there to see!"

Quincy jumped. "Not quite!" she hollered. Yanking down her glasses, she slid off the bed and headed for the door, rolling up her sleeves as she went.

3

The next morning was cold and drizzly. Knowing she would probably be called in to work at Uncle George's umbrella shop, Mrs. Rumpel was up early. Dressing quickly, she hurried downstairs to start breakfast. Outside it was still dark, in the early-morning gloom of a West Coast winter.

In the kitchen she found Quincy sitting at the table eating a bowl of cereal. Propped in front of her was an Agatha Christie mystery.

"Good grief," said Mrs. Rumpel. "You're up early."

"This is great stuff, Mom!" Quincy was wearing a long yellow sweater with a pattern of green frogs. This was matched with green pants covered with a pattern of smaller yellow frogs. Tiny plastic frog earrings dangled from her ears.

Mrs. Rumpel gazed fondly at her eldest daughter. *Quincy was growing up, for sure!* "You look very nice in your new outfit, dear," she said. "Is there something special on today?"

"I'm definitely taking on the Beanblossom case," replied Quincy. "And I want to look professional. I'm going over to talk to Mrs. Murphy before school."

"I don't think you'll be able to. The Murphys never get up this early." Mrs. Rumpel glanced out the window. But just as she spoke, their neighbours' kitchen light suddenly came on.

"That's odd," said Mrs. Rumpel.

Shoving back her chair, Quincy joined her mother at the window. "Well, they're sure up this morning," she said, grabbing her ski jacket off the kitchen floor. "I'm going over there."

Quincy climbed over the sagging wire fence that separated the two backyards, climbed the back porch steps and knocked on the kitchen door. As she waited for it to open, Bilbo Baggins, the Murphys' old striped cat, eyed her suspiciously from his perch on the porch railing.

At last the back door opened to reveal Mr. Murphy, somewhat grizzled, and enveloped neck to toe in a long flannel bathrobe. Clutched in one hand was an empty brown teapot.

"Oh, it's you, Quincy," he said, looking surprised. "Is something the matter?"

"I was just going to ask you that. Your light's on so early."

"Come in, come in," said Mr. Murphy, waving the teapot. "No, nothing is really the matter. Mrs. Murphy just had one of her nights, and we didn't get much sleep." In the background, the kettle whistled shrilly on the stove as Quincy followed him inside.

"Now where did those teabags get to?" As he shuffled about the kitchen, opening and closing cupboards,

Mr. Murphy at times almost disappeared from sight in the billowing clouds of steam from the kettle.

"Ah-hah!" he cried at last. "I found you, you little rascals!" Plopping a teabag into the pot, he poured in the hot water, silencing the kettle once and for all.

"I was wondering if I could speak with Mrs. Murphy," said Quincy, when he was finally able to listen.

"Why, sure, lass. It would probably be good for her. She's still feeling a mite upset. I think it was that pizza she ate last night. It always gives her strange dreams. Will you join us in a cup of tea?"

"Uh, no, thanks, I just had breakfast. Where is Mrs. Murphy?"

"Still in bed, poor wee thing. Waiting for her tea."

"Sometimes Dad takes Mom coffee in bed," said Quincy. "On Mother's Day, usually. And once when she hit her head on the chandelier in the living room and knocked herself out."

Just then a weak voice was heard from upstairs. "Harold, who are you talking to? Bilbo?"

"Not Bilbo, dearest. It's Quincy," said Mr. Murphy, pointing Quincy upstairs to the bedroom, and handing her a cup of tea.

Quincy could hardly believe it was Mrs. Murphy. She was pale and dishevelled, and though propped up with pillows, her arms lay limply on top of the covers. Her ample bosom, hidden under a long-sleeved red nightshirt with the words "Reno Weekend" across the front, rose and fell alarmingly.

"Mrs. Murphy! What happened?" cried Quincy.

"It wasn't anything, dear. Nothing to worry about," quavered Mrs. Murphy, taking a sip of tea.

"But you look awful!"

"It's probably that chili we had for supper last night. I never sleep well after chili."

As she sipped her tea, Mrs. Murphy's appearance began to take a turn for the better. Her normal ruddy colour returned to her cheeks, and Quincy was relieved to see "Reno Weekend" settle down.

"Do sit down, Quincy, and stop staring at me like that." Mrs. Murphy waved Quincy towards a chair heaped with sewing materials. "Just put those things on the floor."

"I can't stay very long, Mrs. Murphy. School, you know. I just wanted to ask you about the Beanblossoms," said Quincy, sitting down gingerly on the edge of the chair.

At the mention of the name "Beanblossom," Mrs. Murphy went pale again. "What did you want to know?" she asked in a shaky voice.

"Oh, anything you know about them . . . the captain and how he died, and the buried treasure, et cetera."

As she said this, Quincy watched Mrs. Murphy closely. Her eyelids seemed to flutter, and her lips trembled as she took another swallow of tea.

"Oh, she's the right one to ask, all right," said Mr. Murphy, bringing in the teapot. "You may as well tell her everything," he said to his wife. "Including the . . . ahem, ghost, ha, ha!"

"Ghost?" cried Quincy. "Is there a ghost?"

26

"*She* thinks there is, but I keep telling her it's just the pizza!"

"But we didn't have pizza last night, Harold. We had chili," said Mrs. Murphy. "And I know I saw it! It wasn't any dream."

"What? What? Tell me about it!" begged Quincy, nearly toppling off her chair in her excitement.

"Well," said Mrs. Murphy, lowering her voice, "I saw it again last night."

"A ghost?" croaked Quincy.

Mrs. Murphy's eyes narrowed. "Captain Beanblossom's!" she whispered.

"Omigosh!"

"In the same place I saw it before. Flitting around in the trees down by his old house. I was just coming to bed after the late late show and Bilbo wanted out, so I let him out the front door. Well! You know how dark it is down by the Beanblossom place . . ."

Quincy nodded.

"Anyway, there was this strange light, and something flitting . . ."

"Ghosts don't flit," interrupted Mr. Murphy.

"This one did," said his wife. "And it sort of twirled. Like a sailor in his hammock. That's how I know it must have been Captain Beanblossom."

"Tell me what happened to him, please," begged Quincy.

Setting down her teacup, Mrs. Murphy plumped up her pillows and settled herself comfortably. "It was a raw February morning, just like this," she began. "The

27

sea-fog was rolling in and the foghorns were moaning. You know, the big foghorn at Point Atkinson that goes, OOOM-PAAA, OOOM-PAAA . . .''

"Yes, I know," said Quincy impatiently. "But what happened?"

"I'm coming to it. It was a morning just like this when the *Molly Flynn* disappeared."

"His ship? Was it hijacked?"

"No. Worse! The *Molly Flynn* was a little boat that the captain used to take out fishing after he retired from the sea. It was his pride and joy, and he would go out fishing in all kinds of weather."

"Alone? Didn't Mrs. Beanblossom go with him?"

"Always alone. She didn't like the sea in any form. She and her little dog, Nanki-Poo, used to watch for him to come back every evening. Or, in the wintertime, every afternoon. They would walk back and forth along the widow's walk . . .''

"I've heard of those!"

'' . . . looking out to sea. The widow's walk across the front of the Beanblossom house had an excellent view, being right on the cliff and all. Well, as I said, one February day, damp and raw, just like today, the old captain decided to go fishing. His wife begged him not to, because he was just getting over the flu, but he insisted. Mr. Murphy is exactly the same. Sometimes he just won't listen to me, even though —"

"I know, I know," said Quincy. "Dad's like that, too. But what happened to Captain Beanblossom?"

"Well, he took a Thermos of soup and some herring strip for bait, and out he went. Didn't matter to him

28

if it was foggy, he said. He had a compass, and he could listen to the foghorns. Anyway, nobody ever saw him again — or the *Molly Flynn*. Just vanished, the both of them!''

''Without a trace!'' marvelled Quincy.

''Well, not quite. A few days later a giant sturgeon was caught in the river, and when they cut it open, guess what they found inside?''

''The captain?'' gasped Quincy, her eyes popping.

''No. A Thermos full of soup!''

''Wow!''

''That's not all,'' continued Mrs. Murphy. ''Mrs. Beanblossom just couldn't believe her husband was gone. Every day she and Nanki-Poo paced back and forth on that little balcony, watching for the *Molly Flynn*. They both got frail and thin. Then, a year later to the day that the captain disappeared, little Nanki-Poo walked right off the end of the widow's walk and crashed into a pot of geraniums below. Right between the rails he went, he was so thin — poor little thing. And that was the end of him!''

Suddenly Quincy thought of Snowflake, and a lump came into her throat. She made up her mind to give him an extra scoop of dog crumbles for supper.

''That's not all, either . . .'' Mrs. Murphy continued. Her eyes had a faraway look.

''Quincy's got to go to school, you know, dear,'' interrupted her husband. ''She can't sit here all day listening to you and these silly —''

''Sure I can,'' said Quincy. ''What else happened?''

"Well, the very next day after Nanki-Poo's fatal fall, their old gardener — you won't believe this — fell out of the apple tree. He was trying to burn some tent caterpillars. And that was the end of *him*!"

"Wow!" Her mind reeling, Quincy got up to go. She couldn't wait to tell Gwen everything she'd learned. But just as she started to thank Mrs. Murphy, she suddenly remembered the main thing she had come to find out.

"The treasure! Do you know anything about a buried treasure?"

"Never heard of any buried treasure around here," said Mr. Murphy, suddenly getting up from his easy chair in the corner. "Now, my dear," he turned to his wife. "How would you like your eggs this morning? Poached, boiled or scrambled?"

"Poached," suggested Mrs. Murphy. "But wait a minute — I'll do them." Seemingly recovered from the shock of seeing the ghost, she sprang out of bed and pulled on a dressing gown. "My stars. I look a fright!" she said, catching a glimpse of herself in the mirror. And with these words, she disappeared into the bathroom.

Quincy went over and stood outside the bathroom door. "Did *you* hear anything about a treasure?" she asked through the keyhole.

"Once, when I first went to see Mrs. Beanblossom in the nursing home, she did say something about a brass monkey, I think it was. But everything in the house was eventually sold at an auction, and no brass monkeys turned up." These words were followed by the sound of water running and much splashing.

"Thanks a lot, Mrs. Murphy," shouted Quincy. "I've got to go now."

The splashing stopped. "You're welcome, dear. Maybe you'd like to go with me to visit Mrs. Beanblossom some Saturday?"

"Oh, gee. I don't know. I'm pretty busy on the weekends." mumbled Quincy.

With these words she departed. Racing downstairs, she zoomed towards the kitchen, unaware she was on a collision course with Mr. Murphy, who was just backing out of the fridge with two eggs. As his knees buckled under him, the eggs splattered to the floor. Quincy's feet shot out from under her, and she found herself sitting in the middle of the Murphys' breakfast.

"Oh, gee, I'm sorry, Mr. Murphy! I'll help you clean up!"

"No, no. It's all right. I'll manage!"

After scooping the raw eggs off her seat with a paper towel graciously proffered by her host, Quincy raced for home and a clean pair of pants. She was almost sure she'd be late for school this time, but she didn't care. The file on the Beanblossom case was now opened.

4

L eah was waiting for Quincy in the front hall, with her jacket zipped up. Her short taffy-coloured ponytails stuck out sideways under her earmuffs. "Quincy! Hurry up! We're going to be late!"

"Oh, boy. Wait till you hear this!" Darting into the kitchen, Quincy got her lunch out of the fridge and shoved it into her backpack, which was still in the corner of the kitchen floor.

"Bye, Mom!" she called out. Then, flinging open the front door, she dashed down the steps with Leah at her heels.

"Mom's gone already," said Leah, struggling to keep up with the long-legged Quincy. "Morris went with her to the bus stop."

"Guess what? Mrs. Murphy saw a ghost last night! She was in a really bad way this morning, you can bet! She's sure it was Captain Beanblossom's ghost because he disappeared at sea in his little boat the *Molly Flynn* on a day just like today and was never seen again except his soup Thermos turned up inside a giant sturgeon!"

"Oh, gee," said Leah, as Quincy paused for breath. "What's a sturgeon?"

"A really big fish. Sort of like a shark. And that's not all. A year to the day later, Mrs. Beanblossom's little dog, Nanki-Poo, fell off the upstairs porch and totalled himself in a pot of geraniums!"

"You mean totalled himself *totally*? Like he died?" gasped Leah.

"He died, all right. And get this . . . the *next* day their very own professional gardener fell out of an apple tree and totalled *himself!*"

"Omigosh!"

"So I guess it's no wonder Mrs. Beanblossom ended up in a nursing home after all that happening," said Quincy. "It's sort of like the mummy's curse or something."

"Quincy, I don't think we should go looking for the treasure," pleaded Leah. "We don't want any mummy's curse on us."

"I was only kidding." By now they had reached Gwen's house. She was waiting out in front in a shiny white raincoat and boots, and equipped with a black-and-white umbrella.

"You're late," she grumbled. "And my hair's gone frizzy. Did you find out about the treasure?"

"I found out more than that." As they hurried towards the school, Quincy retold her story. "I was totally shocked when I saw Mrs. Murphy. She was almost totally collapsed!"

"Maybe it's the mummy's curse," said Leah.

"So now we have a real case with a lost treasure *and* a ghost to investigate," Quincy continued eagerly.

"I don't think I want to be on this case," said Leah.

"That's silly," said Gwen. "There's no such things as ghosts nor mummys' curses, either. But I think we should try and find Mrs. Beanblossom's brass monkeys for her. That would be the humanitarian thing to do."

"Nobody's proved there *aren't* any ghosts," said Quincy crossly. "And haven't you ever heard of the curse of King Tut's tomb?"

"Everybody's heard of that," scoffed Gwen. "But they haven't proved anything."

"Are you sure?" asked Leah. They were at their lockers, and she was glancing nervously at the hall clock.

"Cross my heart," Gwen assured her, looking in the mirror hanging on the inside of her locker door and flattening her hair.

Leah looked relieved. "Is it all right if I tell Morris, then? He'll die if we don't let him come with us."

"Not Morris!" protested Gwen.

"I agree. This is going to be an all-woman investigation. Maybe we'll get into the *Guinness Book of Records*." Quincy's voice was muffled, coming from the depths of her locker where she was rummaging for a notebook.

As they pushed their way through the crowded corridor to their homeroom, Gwen and Quincy checked over some possibilities.

"Of course, brass monkeys don't have to be brass monkeys, *per se*," said Gwen. "It could be the title of a manuscript, or a painting by somebody famous. Maybe it's a picture of the three little monkeys — you know, *see no evil, hear no evil, speak no evil!*"

"Actually," said Quincy, "I'm not sure if she said *monkeys* or *monkey*. There was an awful lot to listen to this morning. I think it's a statue, and it's buried somewhere. Maybe it's really a gold statue, but she called it brass . . ."

The day dragged on, with a brief interlude over lunch when the three girls got together to make plans. "This has got to be top secret," said Quincy. "We don't want the whole school over there digging around."

Gwen and Leah nodded.

"Then it's agreed. We rendezvous at four o'clock, at 57 Tulip Street."

"But that's our house," said Leah. "Aren't we going to walk home together?"

Quincy rolled her eyes. "Of course we are," she sighed. "It's just more professional to say rendezvous, that's all." Scrunching her lunch bag into a ball, she fired it at the trash can. "Remember. Mum's the word."

But at band practice that afternoon, while everybody was listening to Gwen do her flute solo up at the front, Quincy turned around to Freddie Twikenham and whispered, "I won't have much time to practice from now on. I have to work on a case."

Behind his tuba, Freddie's eyes opened in surprise. "What kind of a case?"

35

"Oh, just buried treasure and ghosts and a haunted house," replied Quincy airily.

Freddie whistled softly.

"Yes, it's the biggest case I've ever worked on," said Quincy, nonchalantly polishing her trombone with her sleeve. "Actually, I just want to help poor old Mrs. Beanblossom, and . . ."

Suddenly she became aware that Gwen had finished her solo. Flouncing back to her seat, she glared at Quincy, while the rest of the class stared and Mr. Reed's voice boomed out, "Yes, Miss Rumpel? Would you care to tell the rest of us about your extra-curricular activities?"

Luckily for Quincy, at that moment the bell rang and everyone began packing up their instruments. As they left the music room, Freddie caught up with her as she slunk out the door past Mr. Reed.

"Do you want some help hunting for this treasure?" he asked. "It reminds me of a case my grandpa had once when he was a Mountie . . ."

Freddie stopped talking, and Quincy turned around to see Gwen standing behind her.

"Are you coming?" asked Gwen coldly. "I believe we have a rendezvous."

"Uh, sure. Did you know Freddie's grandpa used to be a Mountie? Maybe Freddie could help us investigate you-know-what."

"I was just telling Quincy of the case Grandpa had once. There was this mad trapper up north who had hidden some gold someplace, but no one could find it till Grandpa got on the case. Anyway, I'd be happy to lend you some Twikenham expertise.''

"I thought this was going to be an all-woman investigation," Gwen said to Quincy.

"Uh, well, I guess we could make an exception for Freddie. He's sort of a professional, with his grandpa being in the Mounties and everything . . .''

"I'm sure it doesn't matter to me." And, tossing her head, Gwen stalked off down the hall.

"Okay, then. We're rendezvousing at my place at four o'clock," Quincy told Freddie.

"Sixteen hundred hours, right! I may as well go with you. There isn't much time for me to go home first." By now Freddie and his tuba had been swept halfway down the hall by the swarm of noisy scholars, freshly dismissed.

"Okay," shouted Quincy. "Meet us outside the east door!''

At the girls' lockers she found Gwen putting on her boots. Gwen didn't speak.

Quincy shoved some books into her locker, then took out her jacket and put it on. "Freddie's walking home with us," she said.

"Well, you certainly are Miss Bossy today, aren't you?" said Gwen, slamming her locker door shut. "Miss General Manager!''

"This *was* my idea, remember?"

In silence, they strode down the hall, one behind the other, to the east door. Outside, they found Leah, Morris and Freddie, with his tuba case. Morris was hopping around impatiently.

"Hurry up, you guys. Let's get started on the treasure hunt!" he squealed. "Chucky's coming, too, but he had to go to the dentist first . . ." And he went bounding ahead of them, arms and legs flailing out in all directions.

"I thought we were keeping Morris out of this," Quincy said to Leah, as the little group straggled out onto the street.

"But he knows all about the Beanblossom place," said Leah. "He and Chucky used to play there."

"Now we've not only got Morris, but Chucky, too," groaned Gwen, marching at the front of the line.

Behind her came Leah and Quincy, with Freddie and his tuba bringing up the rear. Almost as tall as Quincy, in the last year he had lost much of the tubbiness that had earned him his earlier nickname. Shifting his tuba to the other side, he asked, "Have you established your *modus operandi* yet?"

"I was . . . uh . . . thinking of 'Rumpel Gumshoes,' " Quincy said.

"*Modus operandi*," repeated Freddie. "It means method of procedure. A plan."

"I know that!"

"Rumpel Gumshoes! Ha, ha, ha!" cackled Morris.

"It certainly doesn't have much class," said Gwen.

Quincy felt her cheeks getting hot. "Well, then, we'll call ourselves Quincy Rumpel P.I. That stands for Private Investigator."

"Actually it doesn't," said Freddie. "Although most people think so. It really stands for *Private Eye*. e.y.e. It was a Pinkerton trademark."

Quincy gritted her teeth. "And just what is a Pinkerton?"

"Only the most famous detective agency in the world. You mean you've never heard of them?"

"I just forgot!"

"Why do we have to call ourselves after you, anyway?" complained Gwen.

"Well, it was my idea, remember? Anyway, you and Freddie can be private eyes, too. Leah, Morris and Chucky can be associates."

"Well, whoop-de-doo," said Leah. "What happened to our all-woman team?"

The cloak of leadership was beginning to feel heavy on Quincy's shoulders. "Oh, all right," she sighed. "You can be a private eye, too."

When they reached the Other Rumpels' house, Gwen dashed inside to change, emerging shortly in skin-tight jeans, turtleneck sweater, flowered gardening gloves, and high-heeled white boots.

As they got nearer to the Rumpels' brown house, they heard a mournful howling. "Methinks I hear the hound of the Baskervilles." said Freddie.

"We're coming, Snowflake!" shouted Morris, running ahead to get the key from its hiding place under the front door mat.

Lugging his tuba, Freddie followed the others inside. Leah went to change, Morris scurried up to his room, and Quincy disappeared into the basement to get some apples.

As she handed them around, Gwen asked, "Aren't you going to change out of your good school clothes?"

"No time," mumbled Quincy, her mouth full. "It's four o'clock already, and it'll be dark soon."

Morris reappeared, eating a bagel and carrying a broom handle attached to a tin can.

"*What* is *that*?" asked Gwen.

"It's a metal detector. Beep, beep. I made it myself. Beep, beep."

"What you need is a mental detector," said Quincy, opening the door.

"This kid is awesome," said Freddie, shaking his head. Then he opened the door and charged outside, hollering, "Come, Watson, come! The game is afoot!"

And with Leah now outfitted in old jeans and jacket, rubber boots, toque and earmuffs, the investigators, accompanied by Snowflake, burst out onto Tulip Street.

5

"All right, everybody," said Quincy, as the little group swarmed along the street. "Here's the plan. We don't have much time today, so we'll just look around and get the general layout. Familiarize ourselves, as it were."

"As it *were*?" squeaked Morris. "You're sure starting to talk funny. Just like Freddie. And who's this Watson guy he's talking about?"

Freddie groaned. "Hasn't he ever heard of Sherlock Holmes?"

"There are a lot of things he hasn't heard of," said Quincy. "Anyway, if anybody asks what we're doing around the Beanblossom place, we keep quiet about the treasure. Agreed?"

The others nodded, but after thinking about it for a moment, Gwen asked, "What *do* we say?"

"We'll say that . . . uh . . . we're getting sponsors for a balloon race," said Quincy.

"But that's not true." Leah looked worried. "Couldn't we say we're bird watchers? Then we could watch some birds and it would be true."

"I'd feel dumb saying I was going in a balloon race," said Freddie.

"If there was one, Quincy would win it. She's got lots of hot air!" cackled Morris.

"Oh, all right, all right," sighed Quincy. "We'll be bird watchers."

By now they had passed the Murphys' house and crossed the street to the other side, where a crumbling fence of woven bamboo marked the beginning of the Beanblossom property.

Ornamental shrubs, grown monstrous with neglect, reached over and through the fence, as if trying to escape from the shadows that wrapped the twisted oaks and brooding cedars.

"Where's the house?" asked Freddie. "I can't even see it."

"Down the driveway, beep, beep," said Morris, pointing his detector ahead to a break in the fence. As they got closer, they saw traces of what had once been a gravelled driveway. Now overgrown with weeds, it seemed to disappear into the darkness.

With Quincy and Freddie in the lead, they started down it, the decaying leaves muffling their footsteps. Tottering along in her high-heeled boots, slightly behind the others, came Gwen.

Suddenly they heard her cry out. "Look!" Turning around, they saw her pointing to a small marker half hidden in the bushes.

The others hurried back to see. "It's a little lighthouse!" exclaimed Leah.

42

"Oh, it's just a grave," said Morris matter-of-factly. "Chucky and me found it before."

"A grave?" cried the others in unison.

"Yeah. It's even got a name on it, but it's sorta hard to read."

"You mean you guys found a *grave*, and you didn't say anything about it?" cried Quincy.

"Well, we weren't actually sure it was a grave. And if we told, Mom would have had a fit and maybe she wouldn't let us play here anymore."

Going over for a closer look, Freddie bent down and pulled away the dead blackberry brambles.

"It looks like some sort of a cement grave marker, all right," he said. "A small one. And it has letters carved in it."

The others approached gingerly. Squatting down, Quincy peered at the inscription. "It's really hard to read. It must be awfully old."

Gwen brushed some dirt off the base of the marker with her gardening glove. "Look, there's some kind of flower twined around the letters."

"And leaves," said Quincy. "And I see an A and an N together. And there's an O. But I can't make out the rest."

Freddie's lips were moving soundlessly. "Of course!" he cried. "A, N, and O . . . Nanki-Poo!"

"You don't mean . . . you mean Nanki-Poo is buried under here?" gasped Leah. "His little bones and all his little teeth?"

"Maybe he's turned into coral or something," Quincy said soothingly. "You know, like in *'Full fathom five thy father lies, of his bones are coral made . . .* ' Come on, let's go and check out the rest of the place. This isn't getting us anywhere. Lots of people bury their dogs in their yards.''

''Not people that I know,'' said Gwen, struggling to get something out of her pants pocket. ''I think it's worth making a note of this.'' After considerable tugging, she managed to extract a small notebook and pencil. She wrote something down, then squeezed both items back into her jeans.

''That's good detective procedure,'' said Freddie approvingly. ''I usually keep a notebook, too. I just don't have mine with me today.''

''I forgot mine, too,'' said Quincy. ''But one can't always think of everything, can one?''

''I guess you read lots of mysteries.'' Gwen batted her eyelashes at Freddie. ''You sound so knowledgeable!''

''Yeah, I like them a lot. Especially Sherlock Holmes.''

''I like Miami Vice,'' piped up Morris.

''Miami *Vice*?'' scoffed Quincy. ''You're not even allowed to watch it.'' She turned to the others. ''Are you guys coming or not?'' And with that she flounced off, accompanied only by Snowflake.

''I guess we'd better go,'' said Gwen. ''Our commander calls, ha, ha!''

''I'll bet your grandpa had lots of exciting things happen in the Mounties,'' Leah said to Freddie as they followed Quincy. ''Our grandpa used to be a dog-

44

catcher, but he lost his job because he wouldn't pick up any dogs. That is, he'd pick them up, but then he'd drive them home and tell the people to look after them better."

Morris, waving his metal detector as he skittered ahead of Gwen, Leah and Freddie, suddenly came to a halt. "Where did Quincy go? Quincy?"

There was a rustling in the bushes, and a voice replied, "I'm over here. Come and see what I found."

Led by Freddie, the others followed a little trail through the soggy underbrush. They found Quincy standing on a miniature stone bridge, while Snowflake rooted around in the wet leaves below.

"How about this," said Quincy. "I'll bet there used to be a little goldfish pool here."

"How did you happen to find it?" wondered Gwen.

"Snowflake found it. Dogs have a sixth sense about things, you know, so I followed him."

Morris immediately began to work his metal detector. "I'll bet this is where they buried the treasure," he said, whacking at the leaves.

"Hey, watch out!" cried Gwen. "You nearly broke my leg!"

"Hold it!" shouted Freddie. "There's something there." Reaching into the soggy pile of debris, he pulled out a small plaster statue.

"It's a little garden gnome!" cried Leah.

The red stocking cap and blue jacket were stained and chipped, but it was intact. One finger was raised to its lips, while the index finger of the other hand pointed off to the distance.

Gwen pointed to a low pedestal at one end of the ornamental bridge. "I'll bet it belongs on that stand."

"You're right," said Freddie, and he set the little figure upright on its pedestal.

"Get it turned the right way," Quincy told him. "See, there's the place for his feet."

"Why?" asked Leah. "What difference does it make?"

"It just might make a lot of difference! I think this is an important clue." Kneeling down beside the statue, Quincy put her face alongside the gnome's outstretched arm.

"What are you doing?" asked Gwen, looking at Quincy's upraised bottom.

"I'm sighting, of course. To see where he's pointing. Ah-hah! How about that? He's pointing smack back towards the driveway!"

"Towards the grave marker?" said Gwen.

"Then that's where the treasure is buried!" cried Morris.

"Next time we'll bring shovels and start digging," decided Quincy.

"Not Nanki-Poo's grave," cried Leah. "You can't dig there."

"But it's the best lead we have so far," said Quincy. "I think we should go back there and—"

Freddie, however, had other ideas. "Come on, we're wasting time," he said. "I want to take a look in that house." And he strode off, followed by Gwen, Leah and Morris.

"I thought I said we were just going to look around ouside today," said Quincy grimly, barging ahead of them. "Hey, what's that little building?" And she pointed to a small shed covered in blackberry brambles.

"It's an old garage," said Morris. "Chucky and me jumped off the roof once and landed in some skunk cabbages."

"It might be the gardener's cottage," said Gwen. "It's got hanging flower baskets."

"There's only one window, and that's boarded up," remarked Quincy. "The whole thing looks about ready to collapse."

"Nobody's living there now, that's for sure," added Freddie.

"I told you," said Morris. "It's a garage."

"Never mind that," Gwen pointed ahead. "There's the house!"

Grey and silent and with its windows boarded, the old house crouched on the edge of the cliff, blindly facing the sea.

"It's creepy, isn't it?" said Leah, as they got closer.

Freddie hurried ahead to inspect the door. "It's padlocked. It isn't going to be easy getting inside."

"Chucky and me know how to get in," said Morris, popping some bubblegum into his mouth and snapping it.

"How?" chorused the others.

"What'll you pay me?"

"Morris," yelled Quincy, "if you want to be a private eye, you have to share information!"

"But I'm not a private eye. I'm just an associate, remember?"

Too disgusted to answer, Quincy strode off in a huff. "Never mind him," Freddie called after her. "We'll find our own way in."

"Watch out you don't fall off the cliff," yelled Morris, as his sister marched around the corner towards the front of the house.

While Freddie poked around looking for an entry, Gwen brushed off the top step with her glove and then seated herself gingerly. Deciding that this was the safest place to be, Leah sat down beside her as Gwen pulled out her notebook and pencil and proceeded to make notes. Nearby, Morris was beep-beeping as he swung his metal dectector like a samurai's sword over the weed-infested garden. The old house, with all its secrets locked within, remained silent . . .

Then, suddenly, an ear-splitting scream rent the air.

"YEEEEOWWW!"

6

"It's Quincy!" yelled Leah.

"I told her not to fall off the cliff," said Morris. Dropping his broom handle, he raced around to the front of the house, where he collided with Freddie coming the other way.

Clutching her notebook and pencil, Gwen slipped and slid through the long wet grass after Morris. Behind her came the sobbing Leah.

But when they got to the other side of the house, there was no trace of Quincy — only the roar of the sea pounding on the rocks far below.

"Look!" cried Morris. "There are her skid marks." And he pointed to a flattened spot at the edge of the grass.

"She could be drowned!" croaked Gwen hoarsely.

"Or creamed on the rocks down there," said Morris. "She's probably mincemeat by now."

"Waaaah!" wailed Leah.

"Stand back, everybody." ordered Freddie. "I'm going to take a look. This is a job for a professional."

Despite this advice, as Freddie crept forward he was followed by the rest of the investigating team, shuffling along behind him, in shocked silence.

Prepared for the worst, they gathered at the edge of the cliff and peeked cautiously over . . . and into a pair of startled blue eyes.

"Quincy?" they gasped. "Is that you?"

"Of course it's me! Who were you expecting— Princess Diana?" answered a voice crossly.

Perched in the middle of a large clump of wild broom, her face and tangled red hair caked with mud, was Quincy. "Can anybody see my glasses?" she asked, peering around. "I lost them!"

"If you're going to do dangerous stuff like this, you'd better make a will," said Morris. "You can leave your Mickey Mouse alarm clock to me."

Gwen pointed to a pair of pink spectacles dangling from a nearby branch. "There they are." Swivelling around in the bush, Quincy retrieved them and plunked them on her nose.

Above her, Gwen squatted down, pencil poised over her notebook. In her best interviewing voice, she asked, "Would you mind telling us exactly what flashed through your mind while you were slipping off the cliff?"

"Did you see yourself when you were a little baby?" wondered Leah.

"Actually," asked Freddie, "what *were* your last thoughts? I've always wondered about that."

"Well," said Quincy, "a picture did sort of float through my mind—sort of a vision, I guess—of a giant bagel filled with cream cheese and . . . . Hey, here's a little trail going down to the beach. It's really steep, though.''

''An otter slide!'' guessed Leah.

''Maybe it's a pirate path,'' said Morris, ''leading to a buried chest full of money.'' Then he pointed down to a scrap of green cloth snagged in the bushes. ''Hey, what's that?''

Wriggling over on her seat, Quincy picked it off. ''It's just an old headband . . . . Aren't you guys going to help me up?''

''Oh, sure.'' Bracing themselves on the slippery ground, Gwen and Freddie each took hold of one of Quincy's arms.

''Okay,'' said Freddie. ''Everybody heave!''

Nothing happened.

''For Pete's sake,'' he said, ''how much do you weigh, anyway?''

''Never mind! I'll do it myself!'' Digging in her feet, Quincy hauled herself up.

As Freddie examined the headband, everyone crowded around. ''Sometimes little things like this are important, you know,'' he pointed out. ''My grandpa used to say that — ''

''Yeah,'' said Morris. ''Pirates wore headbands. I've seen pictures of them.''

''They wore handkerchiefs,'' Gwen corrected him. ''Or scarves. Not headbands with little tags in them.''

''What does the little tag say?'' asked Leah, trying to see.

"There's an N and an O," said Gwen, "and an S."

"I see a big E!" cried Morris.

"NOSE!" shouted Quincy triumphantly.

Removing his sunglasses, Freddie peered closely at the headband. "There's also an A and a T."

"Eaton's!" cried Gwen, and the puzzle was solved.

"Well," said Quincy, "at least we know *somebody* has been here. And not too long ago, either. Maybe we're not the only ones looking for the treasure."

"In the face of this new evidence, I think we should check the trail more closely." Flopping down on his stomach, Freddie leaned over the edge of the cliff. Suddenly he gave a whoop. "Look at that! There's a footprint, and it's a doozie! A great big one! It's some kind of a sneaker. Wow! I'm going to bring some plaster and make a cast of it!"

"Don't bother," muttered Quincy. "It's mine."

Suddenly Leah whispered, "Shhhhh. Did you hear that?"

Everyone stopped talking. "What?"

"Sort of a *wooo wooo* sound."

"The ghost!" cried Morris.

"Quincy, can we please go home now?" pleaded Leah.

"It *is* getting dark. I can't even see to write anymore," said Gwen, hastily putting away her notebook.

The daylight had nearly gone. Wisps of sea fog drifted in over the bank, wrapping the old house in grey shrouds. From somewhere came the distant moan of a foghorn.

"Look!" cried Quincy. "Up on the roof!"

The little group stared up through the dusk. "It's just an owl," Freddie said.

"A symbol of *death*!" whispered Quincy.

"M-maybe it's the mummy's curse!" quavered Leah, clutching Quincy's arm.

"Nobody told me anything about a mummy's curse," squeaked Morris, his brown eyes growing big with concern.

"There's no mummy and there's no mummy's curse," Quincy insisted. "It's just an old place where we're looking for a lost treasure, that's all."

"Of course, there *was* a mysterious disappearance," Freddie reminded her.

"And don't forget the strange deaths of Nanki-Poo and the gardener," said Gwen.

For a moment everyone was silent, looking around nervously as if half expecting to see the little dog and the old man watching them from the shadows. Then they became aware of a rustling high in the trees above them.

"Listen to that," said Gwen, shivering. "The wind must be getting up. I think we'd better go."

Quincy squinted up into the treetops. "It's birds. A whole bunch of little birds. With . . . uh . . . funny black wings and . . ."

"Those aren't birds," said Freddie casually. "They're bats."

"*Bats*?" Gwen began patting her head frantically with her gloved hand. "What's in my hair? I feel something in my hair!"

"Something fuzzy!" croaked Leah. "Something fuzzy touched my face!"

"I'm getting out of here!" squealed Morris. Picking up his broom handle, he fled. The ranks broke, and the rest of the investigators went skidding and stumbling through the long wet grass after him. By the time they reached the driveway, everyone was jogging in silence.

Suddenly Morris stopped in his tracks. Everyone immediately piled into him from behind.

"What's the matter?" they cried, jostling one another as they sorted themselves out.

"Shhh," hissed Morris, pointing into the bushes. "Over there, behind Nanki-Poo's grave!"

In the shadows, beyond the marker, something was moving.

"Omigosh!" gasped Quincy. Snowflake whined and pressed himself against the back of her legs, while Leah gave a stifled scream and grabbed for the nearest person. It was Morris.

"YEEEEOWWWW!" he hollered. Shaking her off, he bolted up the driveway. Snowflake followed, giving little staccato yelps of panic.

The others stood rooted in fear at a sudden crashing about in the underbrush. There was a rustling of leaves and a snapping of branches . . . then, slowly the noise receded.

"It's going away," whispered Quincy. "Whatever it was, it's going away."

"I'm not staying around here!" said Gwen, and she went wobbling up the driveway as fast as her high-heeled boots would let her. Silently, and with one accord, Quincy, Leah and Freddie sprinted after her.

When they reached Tulip Street, they pounded along in a tight little pack, not speaking until they reached the brightly lit Rumpel house, where Morris had turned on every light.

Finally Gwen spoke. "I wonder what that was back there? an animal?"

"A g-ghost?" stammered Leah.

"Whatever it was, we scared it away," said Quincy, trying to sound reassuring.

"Not *it*." Freddie's voice came out higher than he intended. "Not it — *him*. I think somebody else is looking for the treasure, too!"

"Then there's no time to lose." Quincy was rapidly regaining her composure. "We'll have to come back tomorrow."

"Can't," said Freddie. "Volleyball."

"Well, what about Saturday morning? Early."

"Right," said Freddie. "Saturday morning it is. I've got to split now — see you at school!" And he loped away.

"I'd better go, too," said Gwen. Giving a toss of her hair and a wave of her flowered gardening glove, she set off at a graceful jog.

"What's that white patch on her seat?" wondered Leah, as her cousin's rear end retreated majestically down Tulip Street.

"Her seam split," said Quincy. "Back at the Bean-blossom place."

"Ha, ha! Why didn't you tell her?"

"Because she probably would have gone right home. Gwen's very sensitive about things like that. Anyway, it gave me something to follow, going up that dark driveway!"

7

As they neared the front door, Quincy said, "Now, be careful what you say to Mom, or she might not let us go back."

They pushed open the door and were greeted by the smell of pepperoni pizza and the sound of lusty singing.

"Oh, my darling, oh, my darling,
Oh, my *darling* Clementine!
Thou art lost and . . ."

"Dad's home!" they cried, running into the kitchen.

Mr. Rumpel's voice trailed off as Leah hurled herself at him.

"How did it go on the island, Dad?" asked Quincy, giving him a hug and a peck on the cheek. "Did you get lots of orders?"

"Did I get orders! I tell you . . . I got so many orders that I'll have to bring in more rebounders. And look what I brought for you." Reaching into his pocket, he took out two pink bracelets and handed them to the girls. "They're coral," he said proudly.

"Coral? Real coral?" Putting on her bracelet, Quincy stared at her wrist unbelievingly, while Leah just stood there holding hers, tears welling up in her eyes.

"Don't you like them?" asked Mr. Rumpel, looking worried.

"Dad, we love 'em!" said Quincy, giving him a hug.

"Look what I got!" said Morris, gleefully waving something. "A real dime bank with five dimes in it already. And Dad brought pizzas for supper."

"How about somebody setting the dining-room table? Your mother will be home soon," said Mr. Rumpel. "And you can put out the wine glasses, too."

"Oh, boy," said Quincy. "You *must* have had a good trip!"

Quickly shedding their muddy clothes, Leah and Quincy trotted back and forth with a red checkered tablecloth, plates, wine glasses and paper napkins, and the Rumpels' silver candelabra. Then, at Quincy's insistence, the lights were turned off and the three red candles, left over from Christmas, were lit.

"Mom sure will be surprised," said Leah, as they waited for Mrs. Rumpel to come home from work.

At last Snowflake's ears pricked up, and his tail began to thump. "Ssssh," whispered Quincy. "She's coming."

The front door opened and closed. "Why is it so dark in here?" a voice asked. Then—*BANG! THUMP! CRASH!*

"Surprise!!" yelled the Rumpels in the dining room.

"Help!" hollered Mrs. Rumpel.

"The lights! Turn on the lights!" cried Mr. Rumpel, stumbling into the hall.

They found Mrs. Rumpel sitting in the middle of the floor. Her yellow rain hat was over her eyes, and her legs were sprawled over a large black case.

"Freddie forgot his tuba," cried Quincy, hauling the instrument case out of the way.

"Are you all right, Mom?" asked Leah as they hoisted Mrs. Rumpel back on her feet.

"I think so," she said, shoving her hat back on her head.

"Boy, was that ever lucky," said Morris.

Mrs. Rumpel stared at her last-born. "How, lucky?"

"It was lucky Freddie's tuba was in its case, or you might have dented it."

When Mrs. Rumpel was sufficiently recovered, the lights were once again turned off and the Rumpels proceeded to dine by candlelight. With gusto they consumed the pizzas, washing them down with two bottles of sparkling apple juice.

"So. And what's been going on while I've been away?" Mr. Rumpel leaned back in his chair with a cup of coffee.

Before Quincy could get a word in, Morris took the floor. "My other tooth came out, see?" he said, baring his gums at his father. Reaching into his pocket, he pulled out an assortment of items and began rummaging through them. Finally, from among the screws, rubber bands and bubblegum balls, he extracted a tiny grubby object.

"And here it is!" he said, lovingly rubbing the grime off his tooth.

"Oh, *gross*!" groaned Leah.

"That's a fine tooth," said Mr. Rumpel. Then, turning to his daughters, he asked, "And what have you girls been up to?"

"Dad, something really exciting!" Quincy's blue eyes sparkled. "We've formed a detective agency, sort of. It's called Quincy Rumpel, Private Eye, and right now we're working on the Beanblossom case."

"Oh, yes," said Mrs. Rumpel. "Did you talk to Mrs. Murphy this morning?"

"Did I! Mom, you wouldn't believe what she told me. Did you know Captain Beanblossom disappeared at sea? And do you know who fell off the Beanblossoms' widow's walk a year to the day later?" Mrs. Rumpel shook her head.

"Nanki-Poo!" shouted Leah and Morris.

"Good grief," cried Mrs. Rumpel. "The professional gardener?"

"No, Nanki-Poo, their dog," said Morris.

"And he's buried under the little lighthouse," added Leah. "Isn't that sad?"

"The gardener died the *next* day," Quincy explained. "*He* fell out of a tree, trying to get some tent caterpillars. We went over there after school today to sort of look around, but it got too dark."

"It's really scary around there," added Leah.

"I wasn't scared!" boasted Morris.

"And just where is this little lighthouse that Nanki-Poo is buried under?" Mr. Rumpel wanted to know.

"Oh, it's not a real lighthouse, Dad," Quincy told him. "It's just a little dog grave marker."

"Maybe the treasure is buried near there somewhere, and we're going to find it," said Morris, disregarding Quincy's scowl.

"You shouldn't be snooping on someone else's property," said Mrs. Rumpel.

"It's just to help poor old Mrs. Beanblossom," cried Quincy. "I thought you said we could help her. Don't you want us to help her?"

"Well, I . . . .What do you think, Harvey?"

"I guess it won't harm anything for them to have a look around."

"Well, all right. But be careful. And don't trample on the garden," said Mrs. Rumpel.

"There's not much garden left," said Leah. "You should see it. It's all weeds. And part of it has slid down the cliff."

"Yeah," added Morris, "just like Quincy. You should have seen her when she fe . . . . Ow!"

Morris stopped in mid-sentence as Quincy gave him a swift kick under the table. Jumping up, she began stacking the plates noisily.

"So, Dad," she said loudly. "You had a good trip, eh?"

"Let me tell you about it . . ." began Mr. Rumpel, and Quincy breathed a sigh of relief. Their parents were safely off the subject of the Beanblossom investigation, and she wanted to keep it that way.

* * *

"Mom and Dad looked real romantic sitting there in

the candlelight, didn't they?'' Leah said later as the girls were getting ready for bed.

"Candlelight is very flattering to older people. If Mom was smart, she'd use candles all the time." Already in her orange striped pyjamas, Quincy was busy tucking something away into the farthest corner of their closet.

"What are you hiding in there?"

"Just my frog sweater and pants. I don't want Mom to find them until I get some of the mud off them."

"You'd better wear old clothes next time," advised Leah.

"I've got my outfit all planned, don't worry. I'm going to borrow Dad's new black jogging suit to wear with that headband we found. That should look professional enough."

Switching off the light, Quincy climbed under the covers.

"You know what?" she said after a few minutes of silence. "I've been doing a lot of thinking about old Mrs. Beanblossom. She must miss little Nanki-Poo something awful. If I weren't so busy, I'd take Snowflake over there to cheer her up sometime . . ."

But there was no answer from the other bed — just a slight snore.

Sighing loudly, Quincy snuggled down and was soon asleep herself.

* * *

Little white dogs wearing armbands, and a sinister

gnome . . . all on a Rumpel Rebounder . . . bouncing their way to the edge of a cliff . . . closer and closer . . .

Suddenly Quincy woke up from her nightmare. Small, icy-cold fingers were clamped on her shoulder. She tried to yell, but the sound stuck in her throat.

"Whaazzit?" mumbled Leah, rising slowly to an upright position in bed, the covers draped around her and her eyes tightly closed.

The door to the hall was open, and the light revealed a small figure in rumpled pyjamas standing by Quincy's bed, clutching her shoulder.

"It's me, Morris!" hissed the figure. "Quincy, I just saw the g-g-ghost!"

8

"What?" cried Quincy. "You saw the *what*?"

"The ghost!" repeated Morris, as Leah disappeared under her covers.

"I got up to go to the bathroom and I looked out my window and I saw this funny light in the trees and it was shaped like a ghost!"

Putting on her glasses, Quincy went over to the window and looked out. "I don't see anything."

"Maybe you can't see it from here. My room's closer to the street . . . Quincy, please come and look!"

"Okay, but I think you were probably dreaming." Quincy tried to sound more convincing than she felt.

Leah's quilt suddenly bumped up as she struggled out from under it. "I'm not staying here alone," she said, padding down the hall after the others.

Backed by reinforcements, Morris went bravely over to his bedroom window. "See? It's still there."

Quincy peered out into the blackness. Sure enough, at the end of the street, something was glowing. The winter-bare skeleton of a tree down at the Beanblossom place seemed to be lit with a pale luminescence. *As if something was hanging there, trailing bits of gauze . . .*

"It looks like a mummy, doesn't it?" whispered Morris. "All coming unwound!"

A cold shiver went up Quincy's spine.

"I don't want to look," said Leah, sitting down on Morris's bed.

"What should we do?" asked Morris, as Quincy closed the curtains.

"I don't know." Quincy tried to think. *Like a sailor in his hammock . . .* Mrs. Murphy's words hammered in her head.

"There are no ghosts, are there, Quince?" asked Leah in a small voice.

"No. That is, I don't think so."

"But what about *that thing* we saw in the bushes — behind Nanki-Poo's grave?" Morris was safely back in bed with the covers up to his chin, but his brown eyes were wide with alarm.

"We didn't actually *see* it, did we? We just saw something move . . . I'm going to have another look out the window."

Pulling the curtain back, Quincy opened the window and stuck her head out. In a moment she closed it again. "It's gone," she said. "The light's gone now."

"Whew! That's a relief!" said Morris. "Quince, will you please go downstairs and get Snowflake for me? I'm still kind of nervous."

"I suppose so."

65

"And while you're down there, you might as well bring me up something to eat. Some Bumble Crumbles would be good. Put some raisins on them." And Morris pulled a comic book out from under his bed, plumped up his pillow, and began to read.

"Shouldn't we tell Mom and Dad?" asked Leah, following Quincy downstairs.

"No. It probably wasn't anything, and they might not let us go back there."

The next morning, Quincy, Leah and Morris slept in. When they finally straggled downstairs with puffy eyes, Mrs. Rumpel said, "Do you feel all right? You're all as pale as ghosts this morning." She began feeling their foreheads.

"Mom, there's no such things as ghosts, are there?" asked Leah anxiously.

"Of course not, dear. It's just a figure of speech."

"Oh, maxi-bummer!" cried Morris suddenly.

"What's the matter?" asked his mother, while his sisters looked at him in alarm.

"I forgot to put my tooth under my pillow last night for the tooth fairy."

"Oh, good grief. Is that all. Look, we're wasting valuable time here," said Quincy. "We're going to be late for school." And she dashed around the kitchen throwing some fruit and a muffin into a plastic bag for her lunch.

As she headed for the front door with her trombone under one arm, Mrs. Rumpel asked, "Aren't you forgetting something?"

"Oh, sorry, Mom." Backing up, Quincy gave her mother a quick peck on the cheek.

"That was nice. But I meant that tuba. Aren't you going to take it with you?"

"Oh, darn. Guess I'd better. Darn that Freddie, anyhow." As Leah held the door open, Quincy staggered out with her load.

Gwen was waiting out in front of her house. "You sure looked funny coming up the street!" she told Quincy.

"Well, I don't feel funny. And you wouldn't, either, if you'd seen what we saw last night."

"A ghost!" said Leah.

"The Beanblossom ghost?"

Quincy nodded. "It was just the way Mrs. Murphy described it — sort of like a sailor in his hammock."

"Morris said it was like a mummy all coming unwound," added Leah.

"There are no such things as ghosts," said Gwen. "There has to be some logical explanation. Like . . . well . . ."

"Anyway, are you all set to do some more investigating after school?" Quincy shifted the tuba to her other arm.

Gwen hesitated. "Uh, I thought I'd stay and watch the volleyball game."

"But it's a boys' game! And, anyway, it's only a practice."

"Whatever. I think we should support our school sports."

"Then how come you never come to watch me shoot baskets?"

"I would not define that as school sports, exactly."

Quincy turned to Leah. "How about you, then? Are you coming to work on the case, or are you scared of the ghost, too?"

"Uh, gee, I'd sort of like to stay and watch Freddie play volleyball, too."

"So that's it. It's Freddie." Quincy's eyes blazed. "Well, if you two think he's so great, *you* can carry his stupid tuba!" Thrusting the instrument case at Gwen, Quincy flounced into the school.

At noon she cornered Morris and Chucky in the lunchroom. "Look what I got!" cried Morris, waving a jelly doughnut at her. "I traded Chucky for it."

Beside him, Chucky sat glumly eating his way through one of Mrs. Rumpel's zucchini muffins.

"Do you guys want to work on the Beanblossom case with me after school?" invited Quincy.

"We can't," said Morris. "I lost my tooth at Chucky's this morning and I've got to find it. It's worth real money."

"I can't eat this muffin, Morris," said Chucky, looking at the mangled remains in his hand. "I want to trade back."

"Too late." mumbled Morris, stuffing the last of the jelly doughnut into his mouth.

After school, Gwen and Leah made their way to the gym, where they had their choice of seats. The grade seven boys' volleyball practice did not attract a large crowd.

"That looks like Quincy," said Leah, pointing to a solitary figure sitting on the sidelines.

"What are you doing here?" asked Gwen, sitting down beside her. "I thought you were going investigating."

"I'm going to watch for a few minutes and then I'm going home to help Mom with supper. I think she deserves it."

"Wow, that's a change!" said Leah.

9

"Where is everybody?" asked Mrs. Rumpel, as she dished up two plates of spaghetti.

"No idea." Mr. Rumpel, waiting patiently at the kitchen table, looked hungry.

At that moment the front door banged. "Hi, Mom. We're home." called Quincy, as she and Leah shed their jackets in the hall.

As they helped themselves to supper, their mother asked, "Have you seen Morris?"

"Eewahoo uckys!" mumbled Quincy, her mouth full of spaghetti.

"He went to Chucky's," translated Leah. "To look for his tooth."

The front door banged again, and after a slight delay, Morris appeared in the kitchen. "Good evening," he said, grinning ghoulishly at them. Protruding over his lower lip were two gigantic yellowish fangs.

"Morris, you aren't funny, you know," said Quincy. "You're revolting."

"I couldn't find my tooth, so Chucky loaned me his vampire fangs to put under my pillow tonight for the tooth fairy. They should be worth a lot of money."

"Don't count on it," said his mother.

"Morris, you idiot. You haven't believed in the tooth fairy for years, and you're still trying to cash in on it," said Quincy in disgust.

Morris ignored her. Laying down the offending fangs beside his empty plate, he sat down at the table. "Where's my supper?" he asked.

"In the pot," said Mrs. Rumpel. "On the stove. Go and get it."

* * *

As soon as supper was over and her share of the dishes done, Quincy disappeared upstairs. When Leah went up later, she found her sister hunched over her desk.

"Quincy? Are you all right?"

"Of course I'm all right."

"You're not doing homework on a *Friday*, are you?"

"Don't be silly. I'm designing a business card with our logo." Blowing away some eraser bits, Quincy held up a piece of paper. "What do you think of this?"

"*Quincy Rumpel, Private Fish,*" read Leah. "That's nice. What does it mean?"

"That's not a fish! That's an eye! *Private Eye!*" Studying her sketch critically, Quincy conceded, "Maybe it does need more eyelashes." And she added another row.

"It would be cool to have some crests made, wouldn't it?"

71

"Oh, boy, yes. Any maybe T-shirts, too. Wouldn't they be great?"

"The ghost isn't there tonight," announced Morris, walking in unannounced. He was wearing his Superman pyjamas and eating a cheese sandwich.

"When are you going to learn to knock before you come in here," cried Quincy. "And what are you doing in your p.j.'s so early?"

"I put my fangs under my pillow already. If I go to sleep now maybe Mom will leave the money nice and early — but if I stay up late she won't have a chance. What are you doing?"

"Business. P.I. Business. Go to bed."

"I know a clue!" Morris, finished with his sandwich, took a handful of crackers out of his pyjama pocket and stuffed them in his mouth.

"I'll bet."

"Maybe he does know something, Quince," said Leah. "Chucky and Morris have been at the Beanblossom place more than anybody."

"Okay," sighed Quincy. "So, what's your clue?"

"Will you clean my room for me if I tell you?"

"Good grief! No, I won't. Sometimes I wonder where Mom and Dad got you, Morris."

"Maybe he's an alien," said Leah hopefully.

"I guess I'll tell you anyway," said Morris. "You know how monkeys like to climb to high places? Well, I'll bet the brass monkey is up high, too! In the attic."

"That's it? That's your great clue?"

"Sure."

"That's not a clue," Quincy told him. "That's just a dumb guess. Let us worry about the clues, okay?"

After adding a decorative border of little squiggles to her business card, Quincy tacked it up on her notice board. Then she took her lucky basketball sneakers from her bookshelf and placed them on the foot of her bed.

"Now I won't waste time looking for them in the morning. I told Gwen and Freddie to get here early, but I suppose we'll be waiting around all day for them." Quincy heaved a deep sigh.

"Freddie says it will take all day to search the house," said Leah.

"It won't if the brass monkey is where I think it is — underneath the little stone bridge!"

"I don't want to go in the house and I don't want to dig anything up. I wish I could stay home." Scrunching down miserably in her bed, Leah pulled the covers over her head.

"Come on," coaxed Quincy. "You'll feel better in the morning when the sun shines." Taking off her glasses and turning off the light, she stretched out in bed, hands clasped behind her head . . . . *The powerful muscles in her sinewy legs rippled beneath the smooth black leather pants as Quincy Rumpel, the private eye from the west, led her team of investigators along the danger-ridden trail . . .*

She had been asleep for some time when Leah woke her. "Are you awake, Quince?"

"I am now. What's the matter?"

"I'm worried about the ghost."

Quincy groaned. "Good grief! How can you always manage to find something to worry about?" She turned on the light and put on her glasses. "All right, if it will make you happy, I'll go and look out Morris's window."

"I'm coming with you."

They tiptoed down the hall. Around them, the house was silent. As Quincy opened Morris's door, the light from the hall showed a large white lump on the bed. Snowflake looked at the intruders sleepily.

Quincy padded across the room and opened the curtain.

"Omigosh!" she whispered. "It's back!"

"I'm going to get Dad!" Leah's voice was panicky as she headed for the door.

"No!" hissed Quincy, hauling her back by the seat of her pyjamas.

Suddenly Snowflake slid to the floor with a thud as Morris sat up in bed. "Who's there?" he squeaked. "The tooth fairy?"

"It's just us," whispered Quincy. "That thing is back in the tree again. I think we should go and see what it is."

"Tomorrow, right?" said Leah hopefully.

"No, I mean right now."

"I got it! I got it!" cried Morris, holding up a shiny new coin. "I got a loony dollar!. And the fangs are still here!"

"Never mind that," said Quincy. "Are you coming with us to check out the light?"

"No," said Morris, diving under his covers with the money.

"We won't *do* anything," promised Quincy. "We'll just go past Murphys' to where we can see better. You can carry the flashlight if you want, and we'll take Snowflake."

"*I'd* like to take Mom and Dad," mumbled Morris, emerging reluctantly from his nest.

"Me, too," said Leah.

"We have to solve this ourselves," said Quincy firmly. "Besides, they probably wouldn't even come, and they wouldn't let us go, either. Whereas, if we don't tell them, they can't say no."

"What if Mom gets up and wonders where we are?"

"Okay, worry wart. I'll leave a note, if it will make you feel any better." Trotting back to her room, Quincy quickly wrote out a few lines on a scrap of paper and stuck it on her pillow:

On a case. Back soon. Love.
signed, Q.R., P.I.

She put on her sneakers and Leah put on her fuzzy pink slippers. Then, with Morris clad in his soccer boots and dragging Snowflake behind him, they crept down the stairs. In the front hall they donned jackets over their pyjamas. Then the investigators let themselves quietly out into the night.

"It's getting windy," said Leah as they shuffled along in a tight little cluster behind Morris's wobbling flashlight. "And my feet are cold."

"My everything is cold," shivered Morris.

"You should have worn socks," said Quincy. "Anyway, we won't be long. And it's not even very late. See, the Murphys are still up." But even as she spoke, their neighbours' house went dark.

"The late, late show must be over," whispered Leah.

"I'll bet Mrs. Murphy was watching 'The Mummy's Secret,'" said Morris. "It's all about this mummy that comes alive, and you should see what it looks like. It's face is all sort of runny . . ."

"Never mind!" hissed Quincy. "Look, now you can see the light at the Beanblossom house." She pointed across the street. There it was — the same pale, flickering mysterious light in the tree.

"I see a mummy, and it's moving." Morris's flashlight jiggled helplessly.

"Listen," croaked Leah, grabbing Quincy's arm. "I hear something!"

Clunk. Clunk. Kerboom. The sound was coming from the Beanblossom place. In the same vicinity as the strange, glowing *thing* in the tree.

"Ghost chains!" cried Morris. "I'm getting out of here!"

"Wait!" Quincy clutched at him, but Morris slipped out of her grasp and was gone, taking the flashlight and Snowflake with him.

Clunk. Clunk. Kerboom.

"Come on, Quince — let's go, too," begged Leah.

Quincy hitched up her pyjama bottoms. "Okay!" she said, and the two girls took off.

At that moment, Mr. Murphy opened his front door. "There you go, you old buzzard," he said cheerfully, nudging Bilbo Baggins outside.

But the cat remained frozen on the doorstep, his fur standing straight up and his back hunched. He was staring up the street.

Mr. Murphy rubbed his eyes. Pounding along Tulip Street towards him in a flash of striped legs, came two white sneakers and a pair of fuzzy pink slippers.

"Oh, hi, Mr. Murphy!" called out Quincy as she passed. Leah just waved.

Shaking his head, Mr. Murphy turned to go back inside. But before he could close the door, Bilbo shot past him. The old cat didn't go out again that night.

* * *

Safely back in their own house, the girls crept upstairs. Morris's light was on and his door was open. In the middle of the bed, Snowflake was turning round and round, smoothing out a place to sleep, while Morris stood at the window eating a banana.

"The light's gone now," he said. "Come and see."

"I've seen enough," said Leah, and she went on down the hall.

Quincy went over to Morris's window and looked out. Tulip Street was dark and silent.

"It's a spooky mystery, isn't it, Quincy?" whispered Morris. Returning to bed, he curled himself up in one corner, in the small space left by Snowflake. "Can you leave my door open?"

Quincy nodded. Leaving Morris's door open, she went back to their own room. Leah was not in sight, but there was a large hump in the middle of her bed, and two pink slippers on the floor underneath it.

The note was still on Quincy's pillow. She stuck it on her notice board (in case it was needed again), then took off her glasses, turned out the light, and climbed into bed.

Her heart was still pounding. *This case is getting more and more scary,* she thought. *It's just like when they opened Pandora's box.*

Downstairs, the clock was just striking two.

10

Quincy woke up with a start. An eerie, pale light was seeping in through the window. Downstairs, somebody was ringing the Rumpels' cowbell.

Nobody seemed to be answering it. Without stopping for her glasses, Quincy stumbled groggily downstairs and opened the door. There stood a small figure enveloped in a large army jacket and clutching a plastic shopping bag. "Hi!" it said. "I brought my lunch."

Squinting, Quincy bent down. "Chucky? Is that you?"

"Sure it's me. Morris said we had to come early. Aren't we going to look for the buried treasure?"

"Yes. But not *this* early. You'd better come in and wait. I'll call Morris. MORRIS! Chucky's here!"

In a moment a tousled head appeared over the upstairs railing. "Chucky, old buddy! Oh, boy. Chucky's here, everybody!" screeched Morris.

"Get dressed, Morris," ordered Quincy, settling Chucky on the bottom step with a comic book. Then she went upstairs to get dressed herself.

Bong, bong, bong! It was the cowbell again. "Somebody get the door!" shouted Quincy from the bathroom.

"What is everyone doing up so early?" muttered Mr. Rumpel, as he hurtled downstairs with his dressing gown flapping. Stumbling around Chucky on the bottom step, he leaped across the hall and flung open the door.

"Hi, Mr. Rumpel," said Freddie. "Quincy said to come early. Today's the big day."

"Freddie! Come on in," said Mr. Rumpel. "I didn't . . . uh . . . recognize you in your trenchcoat and hat and sunglasses."

"That's good, Mr. Rumpel — that you didn't recognize me, I mean. It's my disguise. Actually, it's not my trenchcoat — it's my dad's. That's why it's a little long. It's his hat, too."

"Well, it certainly is an effective disguise, that's for sure," said Mr. Rumpel, ushering Freddie to a seat on the stairs beside Chucky. Then he paused. "Actually," he said, "what *is* going on today?"

"It's our big investigation, Mr. Rumpel," said Freddie. "The Beanblossom case. Don't you remember?"

"Oh, yes. Well, don't dig up any wooden nickels! Ha, ha!" Continuing on his way, Mr. Rumpel jumped nimbly aside as Morris came leaping down, wearing a grubby red scarf tied around his head and flourishing his metal detector.

By the time Gwen arrived precisely at eight (wearing roomy rugby pants), Freddie and Chucky were in the kitchen watching Quincy, Leah and Morris eat breakfast. Mr. Rumpel had been reluctant to hand over his new jogging suit, so Quincy was again dressed in her frog outfit, with the matching green headband.

Morris was telling Freddie and Chucky about the ghost. "So I was keeping an eye on the place from my window, and there was this thing — sort of like a flying saucer or a ghost or a mummy — spinning around in the trees. So I thought, I'd better check it out, and . . ."

"Oh, wow," exclaimed Chucky. "Weren't you scared?"

"Nah, not a bit. Anyway, when we got near, it started making this awesome noise — *crash, bang, zaaap! Crash, bang, zaaap!* Just like ghost chains rattling!"

"I would have freaked out!" said Chucky.

"Quincy and Leah nearly did," bragged Morris.

"*Morris*!" Quincy gave him a withering look, and Morris went back to eating his cereal in silence. "Besides, the noise wasn't like that at all. It was more like *clunk, clunk, kerboom . . . clunk, clunk, kerboom.*"

"Do you think Mrs. Beanblossom will give us a reward?" asked Morris.

"Maybe a modest amount," said Freddie.

"Of course, we wouldn't have to take it," Gwen pointed out.

"But what if the treasure is worth *billions*? I'd sure like to get a horse," said Leah.

"Do you know what I'd get?" cried Morris. "I'd get a Ferrari and a trail bike and five hundred dozen jelly doughnuts."

"Well, I don't think we'll get a reward," said Quincy. "But if we did, I wouldn't mind one of those fancy skateboards and a horse and some riding lessons and . . .''

''We'd better get started if we're going at all!'' Gwen interrupted. ''It was getting foggy out when I came over.''

Equipped this time with a shovel and Gwen's bird-watching binoculars, the investigators set out.

''Wow!'' cried Morris. ''Look at the fog! I can't even see the Murphys' house!''

''This must be a real sea-fog,'' said Quincy. ''Just like when Captain Beanblossom disappeared.''

''Maybe we shouldn't go.'' Leah looked at the others hopefully, but nobody seemed inclined to turn back.

''I was thinking about the gnome,'' said Quincy as they groped their way along the street. ''I think when we picked him up we faced him the wrong way. He was really meant to point back to the little bridge. Let's dig there first.''

''It's an idea,'' Freddie admitted. ''However, I've worked out another *modus operandi*. I think we should start by checking the house. Reason: We don't even know what this brass monkey is. It could be old stock certificates, for instance, for a gold mine or something. In which case it would likely be hidden somewhere in the house.''

''That makes sense,'' said Gwen. ''I agree with Freddie.''

''No kidding,'' muttered Quincy to herself.

As they straggled down the Beanblossom driveway under the dripping and ghostly trees, Leah pointed into the bushes. "There's Nanki-Poo's grave." It was barely discernible in the fog.

"We should have a look at Quincy's gnome, all the same," said Freddie. "Just for the record — before we get to the house. Do you want to lead the way, Quincy?"

"Gee, thanks," said Quincy.

"Do you think you can find it in the fog?" asked Gwen.

"Piece of cake," said Quincy. "Follow me." And she plunged off into the underbrush. Behind her came the others, slipping and sliding on the wet leaves.

"Are you sure you know where you're going?" asked Freddie, as Quincy thrashed her way along.

"Sure. It's right in here somewhere. Look, here it is." The little gnome was just as they'd left it, its outstretched arm pointing back towards the lighthouse.

As the others gathered around, Quincy bent down and turned the figure on its base. "See? It works this way, and now it's pointing right at the bridge."

"But it doesn't fit quite as well," said Gwen, examining it carefully. "It definitely points to the lighthouse."

"I'm afraid Gwen's right," said Freddie. "It does. If we don't find anything in the house, we'll have to dig around the marker."

"Oh, poor little Nanki-Poo," moaned Leah.

"Look at Snowflake," said Chucky, pointing to the big dog rooting around at the bottom of the small abandoned pool. Suddenly he began digging furiously.

"He's found the treasure!" cried Morris.

As the investigators stared in fascination, clumps of mud and soggy leaves flew through the air. Faster and faster went Snowflake's front paws. Finally, after much snorting and snuffling, he emerged triumphant, holding something tenderly in his mouth.

"It's gold!" shouted Morris.

Bending down, Quincy stuck her fingers in Snowflake's mouth. "Come on, Snowflake, there's a good dog . . . drop it."

Snowflake's jaws went slack, but he wouldn't drop his treasure. Finally Quincy fished it out of his mouth.

"Oh, for Pete's sake," she said. "It's just an old lid."

"Let's see it." Freddie held out his hand. "It looks like a cover from an old car radiator. If nobody wants it, I'll keep it."

"Good grief, no! We don't want it," said Quincy, wiping her hands on her pants, while Gwen shook her head in horror at the thought.

"I want it!" cried Morris, snatching the cover from Freddie.

"Morris, you give that back to Freddie!" ordered Quincy.

"It's our dog that found it, and I'm keeping it."

"Aw, let him have it," said Freddie. "I've got enough junk at home, anyway."

"Have you got any more junk you don't want?" wheedled Morris, stowing the grimy metal lid away in his pocket.

"Morris, get lost!" yelled Quincy. "Beat it! Go home!"

"You'll be sorry!" And Morris stomped away, followed by the faithful Chucky.

Quincy sighed. "Do you want to do any digging here just in case?" she asked the others.

"No! Remember the bats?" said Leah. She looked up nervously, but the tops of the trees were lost in the fog.

"We might as well get to the house and see what's there," said Freddie. "I brought my skeleton key this time, so we'll get in for sure."

They groped their way back to the driveway and trod down it, their footsteps muffled by the sodden leaves. All at once, out of the fog that swirled around them, loomed the old house.

"It looks spookier than it did the other day," said Leah, as the three girls followed Freddie around to the front door.

"Now we get down to business," he said, taking a key out of his coat pocket. Silently, they watched as he tried to insert it in the padlock.

Freddie groaned. "It won't fit."

"Try the back door," said Quincy, and they trailed around to the back of the house. The key still didn't fit.

"I thought for sure it would fit!" said Freddie.

"Gee, that's too bad," said Leah. "I guess we may as well go home." She turned around and started heading down the steps.

But Quincy, who had her nose pressed against the kitchen window, waved at her to keep quiet. Suddenly she jumped back. Her words came out in a hoarse whisper.

"There's somebody in there!"

11

Bumping into one another in their haste to get away, the four investigators went floundering down the steps. Quincy crashed into Gwen, who crashed into Leah, who crashed into Freddie, who tripped on his long trenchcoat and lost his balance. They all piled together in a heap at the bottom of the steps.

As they scrambled to their feet, the door behind them suddenly creaked open. Frozen in their tracks, they turned and stared at it.

"Ha, ha! You guys!" chortled a squeaky voice. "We sure fooled you!"

Shaking her fist, Quincy took a step towards the house. "So help me, Morris, some day you're going to get it."

The door opened further to reveal Chucky and Morris. "We told you we knew how to get in!" they bragged.

"I suppose you got in through the basement," said Freddie crossly, retrieving his hat from the mud.

"Nope. There isn't any. Come here and we'll show you!"

They trooped back up the stairs and into a kitchen dimly lit by one window. There were cupboards and a counter and a sink.

"Aren't there any lights in here?" asked Leah. "It's awfully gloomy."

"They don't work," said Morris. "Look, there's our secret door." And they pointed to a small panel in the wall near the floor by the back door. "It swings open and shut like this, see? And that's how we got in."

"It's a dog door," cried Quincy. "Nanki-Poo's little dog door. You mean you guys crawled through *there*?"

"Sure. It was easy," said Morris.

"No, it wasn't," said Chucky. "It was tight."

Quincy pushed open a door in the corner of the kitchen. "I wonder what's in here?"

Freddie pulled a flashlight out of one of his coat pockets and shone it in. "It must be a laundry room. See the connections in the wall? They're for a washing machine."

"Oh, is that what they are?" said Gwen. "You sure are good at this, Freddie."

"Huh!" snorted Quincy. "Anybody could have figured that out. Hey, here's an old laundry basket full of stuff." She began rummaging through it and lifted out an old lace curtain. Draping it over her head, she murmured, "Come with me to the Casbah . . ." Quincy sashayed back into the kitchen.

There was no one there. Everyone was in the living room, where Freddie was examining the fireplace. "Look at this — a two-way woodbox,'' he was saying. "If you examine it closely, you will notice that it opens right to the outside.''

"I wish we'd known that,'' said Chucky. "We could have come in that way instead of through the dog door.''

"No, you couldn't.'' Freddie shone his light into the woodbox. "It's bolted from the inside, see? Therefore,'' he continued, "from this we can safely conclude that nobody else can get in, either.''

"Doesn't Freddie talk just like Sherlock Holmes?'' said Leah admiringly. Gwen nodded.

No one noticed Quincy. Swivelling her hips, she flicked her curtain and growled more loudly, "Come wid meee to de Casbaaah . . .''

This time everyone looked. "Ha, ha!'' giggled Morris and Chucky, doubling up with laughter. "Look, it's the bride of Frankenstein!''

"That old curtain may be full of spiders,'' warned Gwen.

"Who's de Casbaaah?'' wondered Leah.

Freddie, immersed in his inspection of the fireplace, merely gave Quincy a quick glance.

Disentangling herself from her lace curtain, she stalked over and joined the others.

"I suppose you noticed there are flowers carved here,'' she said, running her hand over the mantel.

"We already saw them,'' Gwen told her. "They're beanblossoms. The name's there, too.''

Freddie shone his flashlight on the mantel, and Quincy could see the whole carving. The name BEANBLOS-

SOM had been carved in the wood, and an intricate pattern of vines was woven through the letters.

"It looks something like what's on the grave-marker, doesn't it?" she said. "Only this one spells Beanblossom."

"What were those letters on the lighthouse?" asked Freddie. "I forget."

Whipping out her notebook, Gwen began flipping pages. "Here it is," she said. "There's an A and a N together, and then there's an O. That makes Nanki-Poo."

"Not necessarily," said Freddie. "Look at this!" And he traced out the same letters on the mantel.

"You're right," cried Gwen. "The grave-marker could be Beanblossom, too."

"You mean there's a person buried under the light-house?" asked Morris.

"It wouldn't be a person," said Gwen. "I'm sure that wouldn't be legal."

"I wonder why this dust is so white and the dust in the kitchen is so dark?" Gwen was looking at Quincy's white fingerprints on her green jogging pants.

"Yuck! She's got human skin on her pants!" said Morris. "Dust is mostly human skin — I heard that on television. It's just like when you get dandruff and it . . ."

"Morris!" protested Leah, as the others groaned.

"Beat it, you kids!" said Freddie, waving Chucky and Morris away.

A moment later there was a squeal from the kitchen. "Morris found a clue, everybody!" hollered Chucky. "Come and see Morris's clue!"

As they all trooped back to the kitchen, Freddie muttered, "This is the most disorganized case I've ever been on!"

"This had better be good," said Quincy, when they were assembled. "What did you find?"

"Ta-*dah*!" Jerking his arm from behind him with a flourish, Morris held up a chopstick.

"Is that all?" groaned the others.

"There *is* something written on it!" Taking the chopstick from Morris, Gwen read aloud, "*Won-Ton-on-the-Run*. That's in the Mall!"

"I guess the Beanblossoms liked Chinese food," said Leah.

"But *Won-Ton-on-the-Run* only opened last month!"

"You know what this means, don't you?" Freddie held the chopstick aloft. "It means somebody has been here."

"I want to go home," said Leah.

"Not now! This investigation is just getting started!" Behind her pink glasses, Quincy's blue eyes gleamed.

"We're going to look for other clues!" Chucky and Morris took off, heady with their discovery.

"I wish we could turn on the lights." Leah shivered as she glanced around the shadowy front room of the old house. The air was clammy, for the damp grey fog outside was seeping in through the boarded-up windows.

Quincy flicked a light switch on and off. "I guess the electricity's been turned off for years and years."

"That's it!" Freddie cried.

Quincy, Gwen and Leah stared at him.

"Electricity! Of course! The lighthouse isn't a grave-marker at all. It used to be a light for the driveway, with their name on it. Boy, are we dumb!"

"That's what we get for listening to Morris," said Gwen. "We should have known better."

"But if Nanki-Poo isn't buried under the lighthouse, then where is he?" Leah looked around worriedly.

"And there's still the gnome," persisted Quincy. "He could still be pointing to the treasure."

"I've seen lots of those gnomes, and none of them were pointing to a treasure," argued Gwen.

"All right, already!" said Freddie. "I said we'll check it out later. First, let's look for a secret panel." And he began tapping the dark-panelled walls of the dining room.

"What exactly are we supposed to be looking for?" asked Gwen, tapping away obediently.

"Anything that sounds hollow or seems remova-ble," Freddie told them. "This panelling seems aw-fully solid, though. Where are you going, Quincy?"

"I just thought of something." Followed by the other three, Quincy went back to the other room. Going directly to the fireplace, she said, "I think I know why this dust is different."

Kneeling down, she beamed Freddie's flashlight onto the white ashes. "Somebody burned something, and the ashes floated over everything in this room, but not in the kitchen. That's just plain old dust in there.''

''Maybe they burned the Chinese food container,'' suggested Gwen. ''Some real estate person, perhaps.''

''Maybe. Hey, look! Here are some pieces that aren't burnt.'' Retrieving some scraps of paper, Quincy spread them out on the hearth.

''That's not from any kind of food container,'' said Freddie, examining them.

Leah picked up one of the pieces. ''It's a picture of a little bird.''

''She's right,'' Freddie agreed. ''It *is* part of a bird.''

''That's odd. Why would anyone want to burn a picture of a bird?'' mused Gwen.

''And do you know something else?'' Quincy's face went white. ''*These ashes are still warm*!''

''Then not only has somebody been here, but they've been here recently,'' said Freddie. ''*Very* recently!''

12

"Morris and Chucky," whispered Quincy hoarsely. "*Where are Morris and Chucky?*"

"They said something about looking for more clues," said Freddie. "They must have gone upstairs."

"But what if somebody is hiding up there, and they've taken Morris and Chucky prisoner?" quavered Leah.

"I think we'd have heard them holler," said Gwen. "And, anyway, we decided no one could have got in with everything locked from the inside. Also, there's no sign of a car anywhere."

"Yes, but what about those warm ashes? Somebody had to make them." Suddenly Quincy slapped herself on the forehead. "Of course! The path from the beach. They didn't use a car—they came up the path. And crawled in through the woodbox!"

"But it's locked," said Leah. "We all saw it was locked from the inside!"

"That's just it. *From the inside*. Don't you see, somebody could have crawled in from outside and *then* locked it."

"That means they could still be in here!"

The words came out in a hoarse whisper as Freddie dropped to his knees in front of the woodbox. Shining his flashlight over the floor, he picked up a few blades of wet grass and a small clump of mud. ''Somebody came in here, all right, and not too long ago!''

''What do we do now?'' asked Gwen.

''We have to find Morris and Chucky before it's too late,'' whispered Quincy.

''That means searching the upstairs,'' Freddie told her.

Quincy looked at the winding stairs leading up to even darker regions of the house. ''I know.''

''Oh, boy,'' moaned Leah. ''I knew we shouldn't have come!'' With her knees knocking together like castanets, she followed the others towards the stairs.

''Maybe we could try calling before we go up there,'' suggested Gwen, looking at the cobwebs in the shadowy corners.

''*Morris!*'' hissed Quincy in her loudest whisper. ''*Chucky!*''

There was no answer.

''Okay, then. Here goes!'' Hitching up her jogging pants, Quincy began to climb the creaky wooden stairs. Close behind, in a tight little pack, came the others. All around them the old house waited, as if it were silently watching them.

Upstairs, the first room they came to was the bathroom. Sitting in the middle of the floor, looking extremely worried, was Snowflake.

''Snowflake! I'd forgotten all about you!'' cried Leah, hugging him. ''Where's Morris?''

He was not in the bathroom, that much was certain. There was a sink, a toilet, a built-in laundry hamper and a medicine cabinet with a mirror. There was also an old-fashioned bathtub with claw feet.

"I've always wanted a bathtub like that," said Quincy, as Gwen paused in front of the mirror to check her hair.

The next room was small, with faded wallpaper. It was totally empty.

So was the last room. It was large, and on its wallpaper, sailing ships floated on a pale-blue sea. There was an adjoining walk-in closet, and French doors leading to a balcony outside. There was no sign of Morris and Chucky, or anybody else.

"That's the widow's walk out there," Quincy pointed out. "And those doors are locked from the inside, too." Opening one, she looked out into the fog. "This is where Mrs. Beanblossom used to walk back and forth, watching for the *Molly Flynn*."

"And that's where poor little Nanki-Poo went to doggy heaven," whispered Leah.

"Why are we whispering?" demanded Gwen. "It's obvious there's no one here."

"But we still haven't found Morris and Chucky," said Quincy. "Where on earth could they be?"

Freddie pointed to the ceiling. "Up there, maybe."

"Up there?"

"Yes. It's the only possibility left. Old houses like this always have attics, perhaps accessible through a closet . . ."

"Like ours!" cried Leah.

"Possibly. I will now proceed to check this one more closely." Freddie shone his flashlight around the large walk-in closet. Almost the size of a small room, it had shelves along one side. At the back was a ladder leading to a trapdoor in the ceiling.

"This is a great closet," said Gwen. "I wouldn't mind one like this. You could keep all your shoes and stuff over here, and put a full-length mirror on that—"

"Look at Snowflake!" cried Leah suddenly. "His nose is twitching! I'll bet Morris and Chucky are up there!"

"They're probably hiding up there to scare us," guessed Quincy. "Morris! Chucky!" she hollered. "Are you up there? You'd better come down, you little air-heads, if you know what's good for you!"

There was no answer.

"Ha! We'll soon find out if they're up there or not." Grabbing hold of the ladder, Quincy began to climb up.

As her sneakers groped for the rungs of the ladder in front of his face, Freddie conceded, "She's got a lot of spunk, for a girl."

"She knows Mom will kill her if she loses Morris," Leah explained.

The palms of Quincy's hands were sweating now. Maybe this was a dumb thing to do. But they *had* to find the little boys. Suddenly she was aware of someone behind her. She turned and looked down. Freddie was following her up and, plodding gamely behind him, came Gwen and Leah.

Quincy grinned down at them. *This is what it's all about*, she thought. *This is the real stuff—friendship and family. One for all, and all for one.* Bolstered by this rush of emotion, she reached up and pushed open the door over her head.

It swung open, and Quincy bounded up into the attic. "All right, you guys! We found you!"

One by one, Freddie, Gwen and Leah scrambled up behind her. As Freddie beamed his flashlight around, there was a sudden flurry of movement in one corner.

"You little twerps have done some dumb things," continued Quincy, "but this takes the cake. Wait till Mom hears about this."

As she spoke, a figure began to emerge from behind some boxes. Quincy felt the hair on the back of her neck prickle. Leah screamed, and Freddie's flashlight fell clattering to the floor.

"Morris?" croaked Quincy hopefully. "Is that you?"

But deep down, she knew it wasn't.

13

"Quick, Ernie. The lantern," cried a raspy voice. "Right! Oops, sorry! I dropped the matches," another voice replied.

Then there were various grunts and groans, and the sound of someone groping on the floor. It was difficult to see anything in the dim light that filtered in through the small skylight in the roof.

Stiff with fear, the four investigators huddled together, staring in horrified fascination as a shadowy figure slowly rose from the floor.

"Ha!" it exclaimed. "Gotcha!"

As Leah screamed, there was the sound of a match being struck. Then the flickering light of a kerosene lantern illuminated the attic.

There were shoe boxes everywhere. One on top of another, they were stacked in piles all over the attic. A giant-sized bamboo basket overflowed with crumpled-up paper. The lantern itself swung from a hook in the rafter, directly above an ancient kitchen table. At one end of the table, a raincoat covered something lumpy. At the other end was a container marked "Won-Ton-on-the-Run." Thumb-tacked to the rafters overhead were dozens of drawings of robin-like birds.

The lighter of the lantern stood behind the table. Short and plump, and wearing gold-rimmed glasses, he was dressed in a rumpled green jogging suit with a white stripe down the leg. His head was bald and shiny.

His companion, in a red jogging suit, was tall and skinny. His matching headband came down nearly to his bushy black eyebrows. He had bushy black hair and a pointed grey beard.

Summoning up her courage, Quincy asked, "What have you done with Morris and Chucky?"

"Don't tell us there are more of you," groaned the tall one.

"You mean you haven't seen them? Two little guys? One's got a broom handle with a tin can on the end, and the other has a plastic bag with his lunch in it . . ."

"Nobody's here but us. Right, Bert?" said the plump one.

Bert shook his head mournfully. "Not till now, Ernie!"

"What are we going to do, Bert? I guess it's curtains for us now."

Suddenly Leah's shoulders started to shake. She gasped and spluttered, and for a moment seemed in danger of choking. Everyone stared at her. "I can't help it," she wheezed.

"What's the matter with you?" cried Quincy, whumping her on the back.

"*Bert and Ernie!*" gasped Leah. "They're called *Bert and Ernie!*" And she collapsed into helpless giggles.

Bert glared at her.

"She didn't mean anything, honest," pleaded Quincy. Then, to her dismay, she began to giggle, too, snorting helplessly.

Bert and Ernie ignored her. "Our cover may be blown," said Bert, "but there is still wind in our sails. We just need a new *modus operandi.*"

"We've got one of those," Leah managed to stammer out.

"It took such a long time to find this place," sighed Ernie, sinking onto a broken kitchen chair. "It was perfect."

"Yes, until these *persons* butted in. Don't you know you're trespassing?" Bert glowered at Quincy.

"Who, moi?"

"Yes, you. And your friends, too. You shouldn't come snooping around where you don't belong."

"But you don't . . ." Quincy started to say, and then thought better of it. "We're sort of private investigators, and . . ."

"Private investigators? Oh, my heavenly days! We're ruined now for sure!" cried Ernie.

"We were investigating . . . uh . . . a ghost for a Mrs. Murphy," Quincy said. "She thought she saw one flitting around in the tree. Actually, we thought we saw one, too. Well, not actually *all* of us. Not Gwen and Freddie. Just Morris and Leah and me. And then we heard this clunking noise last night . . ."

101

"Oy! A clunking noise!" cried Ernie. "They heard us, Bert! I told you somebody would hear us!"

"That was you?" gasped Quincy. "And was that you in the bushes the other night? By the driveway?"

Bert nodded sadly. "That was Ernie. He was feeling pale, and went out for some fresh air. But something scared him, so he hurried back in. Anyway, we're all washed up now." He sagged weakly onto the other kitchen chair. "We're water under the ducks. Our pie in the sky never got out of the oven. Our golden goose didn't get a chance to lay an egg. And all because of you."

"We're sorry if we caused you any trouble," said Quincy.

"Maybe it's not so bad," said Ernie. "Maybe we can start somewhere else."

"We will, never fear. We'll rise again, like phoenix from the barbecue!" declared Bert.

"Then it's all right if we go now?" Gwen began to zip up her jacket.

"I didn't say that," said Bert. "Sit down!"

"On the floor?" Gwen looked around in dismay. There were no more chairs. Finally she took a Kleenex out of her pocket and sat on that. Quincy, Leah and Freddie sat down in a row beside her.

Just then a mournful wail was heard from below.

"What's that?" Bert jumped up in alarm.

"Police? Oh, good heavens, no!" cried Ernie.

"That's Snowfang, the Rumpels' *vicious* hound," Freddie told them.

"Is that all?" Ernie sighed with relief. "I just love dogs! What kind is he?"

"He's sort of a spotted Samoyed," Leah explained.

"Oh, one of those," said Ernie. "I had a fluffy Dalmation once . . ."

"Ernie, this is no time to be discussing dogs," Bert interrupted. "We are at a chrysalis in our lives, and it's all your fault. If you had learned to draw proper robins, we wouldn't be in this pickle."

"I just need a little more time, Bert, I promise." Picking up the Won-Ton-on-the-Run container, Ernie began to poke at it with a single chopstick. "I hope you young people don't mind if I eat my lunch. I didn't get any breakfast this morning, because *he* was in such a hurry!" He waved the chopstick at Bert.

"You should never skip breakfast, you know," said Gwen. "It's the most important meal of the day."

"Did you draw those birds?" asked Leah, pointing to the pictures on the rafters. "I just love them!"

"Thank you. It's too bad somebody else doesn't like them." Ernie rolled his eyes towards his partner.

"We found bits of bird pictures in the fireplace downstairs," said Freddie. "They'd been burned."

"I know. And *he* did it! And they weren't just pictures . . . those were genuine proofs. The real thing. Only Bert didn't think they were good enough."

"Proofs? The real thing? Robins?" cried Freddie. "This is highly significant! It would seem you are discussing counterfeit money!"

"Is he with the Revenue Department?" asked Bert, looking at Freddie in his dark glasses, trenchcoat and snap-brim hat.

"It doesn't matter, anyway. The cat is cooked. Our goose is finally out of the bag. We are finished," moaned Bert. Pushing back his chair, he made his way over to the shoe boxes. Sighing heavily, he picked one up and put it on the table. "Just take a look in there."

As he swooped off the lid, the investigators scrambled to their feet. "Wow!" they cried, crowding around the table.

The box was stuffed with money. New money. Brand-new Canadian two-dollar bills, with pictures of strange-looking birds on them.

"Did you steal it?" asked Gwen.

Ernie and Bert looked shocked. "Of course not. We wouldn't do anything like that. We made it ourselves."

"It's . . . uh . . . very good," said Quincy politely.

"No, it isn't." Bert shook his head sadly. "Just look at those robins . . . they're terrible. And *he* said he could draw!" And he picked up a handful of the bills and passed them around.

"I suppose they are a little large for robins," Freddie admitted, studying them.

"And they're quite red, too," added Gwen. "Robins are more orangey."

"They look something like giant chickadees," decided Quincy. "Only with longer legs."

"There, I told you they were no good," Bert said to Ernie.

"It's not as easy as it looks, you know, getting their little smiles just right." Ernie was still trying to scoop up some chow mein with his chopstick.

"But how did you do it?" asked Freddie. "You'd have to have a printing press and everything."

Smiling modestly, Bert whipped the raincoat from the table. Underneath was a small printing press. "It's kind of a noisy one," he said, "But it does the job."

"Noisy is right," said Ernie. "Clunk, clunk, kerboom! It drives me bananas."

"Clunk, clunk, kerboom?" cried Quincy. "That's the noise we heard last night."

"We *were* working late last night," admitted Bert.

"We thought it was ghost chains!" said Leah.

"Have you done this much? I mean, do you do this for a living?" Gwen asked.

"We've *never* done it before!" Ernie looked indignant. "We just thought we'd try it. We work in a shoe store usually. That's where we got all the boxes."

"And that's why we have to work here at night. Or at least we *did*, before we were discovered." Bert glared at the four investigators accusingly from beneath his bushy black eyebrows.

"Never mind, Bert," said Ernie. "I'll practise my robins, and then we'll start over again, someplace else."

"You mean you're going to go on doing this?" Gwen looked shocked.

"But you shouldn't. It's very wrong!" cried Leah.

"But we wouldn't be hurting anybody," said Ernie, who was beginning to look a little worried.

"What about your grandchildren?" asked Quincy. "You'd be hurting them. What if you have to go to jail?"

"The law does not view counterfeiters lightly, you know," said Freddie sternly.

Ernie's lower lip began to tremble. "I'd hate little Ernestinc to bc disappointed in me," he admitted, his eyes filling with tears.

Bert's bushy black eyebrows were working violently up and down. "I only wanted to buy some nice things for little Albert," he said, blowing his nose with a loud honk. "Everybody says he looks just like me, you know."

Suddenly Ernie cried, "Let's do it! Let's go straight! No more funny money!"

"We'll burn the whole kit and kaboodle!" declared Bert. Jumping up from his chair, he began taking robins down from the rafters.

"We'll help you carry everything downstairs," offered Freddie. "Then you can burn the money in the fireplace." Picking up the basket of discarded robin drawings, he stumbled over to the ladder.

Beaming delightedly, as if a great weight had been lifted from his shoulders, Bert leaped around the attic in his red jogging suit, gathering up shoe boxes.

"You're going to have trouble getting down the ladder with those," said Quincy. "Why don't we go down first, and then you can pass them down to us?"

"Good thinking!" cried Bert.

Gwen, Leah and Quincy climbed down the ladder after Freddie. Then Ernie and Bert began passing down the shoe boxes of money. Last of all, they struggled down with the printing press.

"Whew!" grunted Ernie, as they set it down on the floor below. "I'll be glad to stop moving *this* around!"

"I just had an idea, Ernie, old pal," said Bert. "What do you think of going into the birthday card business?"

"Selling them?" Ernie looked doubtful. "I'm not even very good at selling shoes . . ."

"No, no. Making them!"

"Making birthday cards! Oh, boy! And get-well cards, and valentine cards, and happy grandfather's day cards and...we'll do them all!" cried Ernie. His round face was wreathed in smiles. "You should see me draw roses! I can draw the most beautiful—"

"Ssssh!" whispered Quincy suddenly. "Somebody's coming!"

14

As they listened, they heard footsteps below. Then a shrill little voice piped up, "If we make a big bust, will Chucky and me get a reward?"

"Oh, no," gasped Quincy.

Then came the sound of many footsteps clumping up the wooden stairs. All at once the room was filled with policemen. Close behind came Morris and Chucky, with Mr. and Mrs. Rumpel bringing up the rear.

"Ha!" roared the sergeant. "Caught you in the act, have we?"

Leah screamed and dropped her shoe boxes. Out flew hundreds of bright new two-dollar bills. Like leaves in autumn, Ernie's red robins whirled through the air, then settled in a little pile on the sergeant's black boots.

"My babies!" cried Mrs. Rumpel, rushing towards Leah and Quincy with outstretched arms.

"I'm sorry, madam." The sergeant motioned to two of his men to halt Mrs. Rumpel's advance. "It appears we have a serious felony here, and we have to get to the bottom of it." He bent over to scoop up a handful of the bills.

"These robins are all wrong!" he said.

"I know," said Ernie, hanging his head. "I just need more practice."

"These are obviously counterfeit bills," continued the sergeant. "And not even good ones. In fact, they are the worst counterfeit bills I've ever seen."

"You don't know how hard it is to get them just right," cried Ernie. "If I just had more time to—"

"You'll get time, all right. Lots of it. In jail—the whole kaboodle of you."

"But they're only babies!" yelled Mrs. Rumpel.

"Sir, these children are innocent!" cried Bert, his eyebrows bristling angrily. "I demand you let them go!" He looked just like the little red devil on the tin of ham, Quincy thought to herself.

Then Freddie spoke up. "Sir, we were just helping them carry their stuff down to the fireplace. I'm Freddie Twikenham, and my grandpa was a Mountie."

"And I'm Gwen Rumpel, officer. My daddy owns the Brolly Shoppe—you've probably heard of him. He's never had a speeding ticket, although he did park twenty minutes in a fifteen-minute zone once. But he put an extra nickel in. I can vouch for these good men. They're going to go straight—they promised."

"They're going into the birthday card business," said Leah. "Ernie's really good at doing roses."

Ernie blushed modestly. "Well, *pretty* good."

"How can I believe you guys will really go straight?" asked the sergeant, his voice not quite as gruff as before.

"Because of little Albert and little Ernestine," cried Quincy. "Because Bert and Ernie are grandfathers."

109

"Well . . ." The sergeant still looked doubtful. "But I'd still have to book you all on breaking and entering."

"Morris let us in," Leah told him.

Everybody looked at Morris and Chucky. "We didn't break anything," said Morris. "Honest! We just crawled in through Nanki-Poo's dog door."

The sergeant sighed. "And what about you two?" he asked Bert and Ernie. "I suppose you came down the chimney."

"Oh, no, your honour! We came in through the woodbox."

"Why has no one ever seen your car?" asked Mr. Rumpel.

"Oh, we don't have a car. We jog. It's much healthier," explained Bert.

"We jog along the beach," said Ernie. "Then we climb the trail and come in through the woodbox."

"Then this is probably yours," said Quincy, taking off the green headband. "I found it on the trail."

"Oh, my, yes. Thank you. I really need that!" cried Ernie, promptly installing it on his shiny head.

"Enough of headbands!" cried the sergeant. "Do you promise not to enter houses through their woodboxes, ever again?"

"Never again!" chorused Bert and Ernie.

"Well, all right," sighed the sergeant. "You can go this time. But we have to confiscate the money and destroy it. Also the printing press and the plates . . . just to make sure you aren't tempted again. Now, what about all you young people. What are you doing here, anyway?"

"We were looking for Mrs. Beanblossom's brass monkey," explained Quincy. "You see, she really needs the money."

"But the only thing we've found so far is an old radiator cover," said Freddie, as Morris pulled the grubby metal lid out of his pocket.

"They haven't made these in a long time," the sergeant said, examining it closely.

"Brass monkey? Did somebody say *brass monkey*?" asked Ernie. "Old Dr. Flooglemeyer used to have one of those."

Everybody stared at him. "What was it?" cried Quincy.

"It was beautiful." Ernie had a faraway look in his eyes. "The brass was all shiny, like gold . . ."

"Yes, *but what was it*?" chorused the Rumpel investigating team.

"Why, a car, of course. Every boy in our town back on the prairies used to dream of owning a car like that. It was just like a Model T, except for the top of the radiator. *That* was all brass, with a screw cap, just like this."

"A vintage car like that would be worth a lot today," said Mr. Rumpel.

"That's it!" Quincy's eyes were sparkling. "That's the brass monkey Mrs. Beanblossom talked about — a car! That's the treasure!"

"But if it is, then where is it?" wondered Freddie. "We've been all over the grounds . . ."

"Maybe it's in the garage," said Morris.

Everybody looked at him. "What garage?"

"You mean the gardener's cottage?" said Gwen.

"I told you it was a garage, lots of times!" answered Morris, crossly.

"Let's go and see this building, whatever it is," said the sergeant. With Morris and Chucky leading the way, everyone trooped outside.

"You're right. It doesn't look much like a garage," said the sergeant when he saw the small, boarded-up, bramble-covered structure with the hanging baskets. Using Quincy's shovel, he wrenched off a board from the cobwebby window and peered inside.

"Well, I'll be . . .!"

Bobbing up and down behind him as they tried to see over his shoulder were Quincy, Gwen, Freddie, Leah, Bert, Ernie, Morris, Chucky, and the Rumpels.

"It's a brass monkey!" cried Ernie. "It is!"

Pressing his nose against the window, Mr. Rumpel said, "It seems to be in good condition, too, except for a missing radiator cap! And Morris can supply that, can't you, Morris?"

"Dad!"

"Hand it over."

"Gee! No reward, no radiator cap, no nothing," grumbled Morris, reluctantly handing the cap to the sergeant.

"We'll have the car moved somewhere for safe-keeping right away," said the sergeant. Then, turning to Morris, he asked curiously, "Tell me, why were you so sure this was a garage? It doesn't look like one."

"Because it smells like one," said Morris.

Everybody sniffed. "He's right, you know," said Mr. Rumpel proudly. "It does."

"Then, if the brass monkey is worth quite a lot of money, Mrs. Beanblossom won't have to worry anymore, right?" asked Quincy.

"Not about money," said her mother. "But she might still be lonely."

"I've been thinking about that, and I've made up my mind. Snowflake and I are going to visit her!"

"Me, too," said Leah.

"Can I come?" asked Gwen.

"Why don't we all go?" cried Quincy. "I'll bet she'd love to see the team that found her brass monkey!"

"Morris and Chucky, too? And Freddie?" Gwen looked doubtful.

"If they want. We'll go tomorrow, and we'll take her some bagels!"

By now the shoe boxes and printing press had been loaded into the police cars. As they drove away, Bert shook his head sadly and gazed up at the big old house. "I wonder how we'll do our birthday cards now?" he said. "We'll have to find a new office."

"Actually," said Mr. Rumpel, clearing his throat, "I've been thinking of expanding . . ." He wiggled his eyebrows at Mrs. Rumpel.

"I suppose we could fix up the basement . . ." she murmured.

"What would you think of the name 'Rumpel Enterprises'?" asked Mr. Rumpel.

"Oh, Dad!" cried Quincy. "You mean we might go into the birthday card business with Bert and Ernie?"

"Well, to start with, we could give them a place to operate from. Would that help you fellows?" And he handed them a card with the Rumpel address on it.

"Sir, you have given us a ray of hope. Perhaps we will still find our pot of honey at the end of the rainbow. Maybe our bridges aren't all burnt, after all!" said Bert grandly.

"We'll be there tomorrow," promised Ernie. "Now I'm going home to practise my roses."

"Thank you, dear young people!" Sweeping off his red headband, Bert bowed deeply. "You have saved us from a life of crime. Little Albert and Ernestine will be forever in your debt!" And giving a last cheerful wave, Ernie and Bert jogged away into the mist.

* * *

By now the fog was lifting, and the sun was trying to come through. "Let's all go home and get some lunch," said Mr. Rumpel. "I'm famished."

"Thanks, Mr. Rumpel. That would be most welcome," said Freddie. "This has been a most surprising investigation — a regular three-pipe case!"

"I'm still worried about the ghost," said Leah.

"I've figured that out," said Quincy. "Come with me." And she led them around to the side of the house. "There, look up in that apple tree."

114

Everybody craned their necks to see. "Ugh," shuddered Gwen. "It's got a gigantic caterpillar nest in it."

"Exactly. That's the ghost. When Bert and Ernie's lantern shone out through the skylight in the attic, it lit up the nest!"

"Awesome!" mumbled Chucky, gulping down the last of his sandwich.

"Aren't you coming to have lunch with us?" Mrs. Rumpel asked him.

"Sure," replied Chucky. "That's why I'm hurrying."

As they went up the winding driveway, Quincy turned to Morris. "Now tell me. How did you and Chucky disappear so fast? And how come you brought Mom and Dad and the police?"

"We were hiding from you in that big closet upstairs — in the room with the sailboats on the walls — because we were going to jump out and scare you guys. Then we heard those guys talking up in the attic, and we got scared. At least, Chucky got scared. So we got out of there as fast as we could and ran home to tell Mom. We thought you were going to get kidnapped!"

"But how did you get out without us seeing you? You sure didn't go down the stairs!"

Chucky and Morris looked at each other and grinned. "We went down the laundry chute!"

"Laundry chute? We didn't see any laundry chute."

"It was right there in the bathroom," explained Morris patiently. "Underneath the clothes hamper. We just climbed in and slid through — and plopped right into the laundry basket downstairs.''

"It was a hoot!'' said Chucky.

I wish I could have done that, thought Quincy. "I'll bet it was!'' she sighed.

Also by Betty Waterton

Quincy Rumpel

Quincy Rumpel wants pierced ears, curly hair, and a Save-the-Whales T-shirt.

Her sister, Leah, can't see why she shouldn't have pierced ears, too, while Morris, her brother, longs for a dog.

Mrs. Rumpel hopes for rain, so her job at the umbrella shop will thrive.

And the neighbours, the Murphys, just can't decide whether having the Rumpels next door is the best or the worst thing that ever happened to them.

ISBN 0-88899-036-7 $5.95   paperback

Starring Quincy Rumpel

About to enter grade seven, Quincy Rumpel is determined that this is the year she will make her mark on the world and become a star. As Mr. Rumpel tries to market his latest business venture, the Rumpel Rebounders, Quincy embarks on a grand plan to advertise the rebounders on television and ensure stardom for herself at the same time.

In this sequel to the enormously popular *Quincy Rumpel*, the whole eccentric clan is back in the rambling house at 57 Tulip Street — Leah, Morris, Mr. and Mrs. Rumpel, cousin Gwen and the Murphys. They are joined by crazy Auntie Fan Twistle and Quincy's latest heart-throb, Morris's soccer coach, Desmond.

ISBN 0-88899-048-0 $5.95   paperback